When We Fell Down

The Seattle Sound Series
Book 7

by Alexa Padgett

When We Fell Down © 2017 Alexa Padgett

Edited by Deborah Nemeth and Nicole Pomeroy
Cover Art by Sarah Hansen of Okay Creations

ISBN: 978-1-945090-20-2

Also by Alexa Padgett

The Seattle Sound Series
Sweet Solace
Between Breaths
Hold You Close
Many Sounds of Silence
From the First
Striker's Waltz
When We Fell Down
A Moonlit Serenade
Moonshine Eyes

The Echo Series
The Spirit Seducer
The Magician's Ruins
The Curse of Kuskurza
Demons & Ultimatums

For Chris. Always.

CHAPTER ONE
Ella

Jeremiah clutched my hand, beaming with pride. We watched the fans, all wrapped up in winter gear, cheeks red from the wind that tunneled into the outdoor venue, clap and cheer for the song Simon wrote for Jeremiah's birth.

"He sounds great," Jeremiah said with a grin. He raised his shining eyes to his father, who was on the stage set up in the middle of the large field. I shivered, surprised by the chill here in Georgia.

"Indeed. Better than ever." Bittersweet, this moment. Selfish though it was, I preferred Simon gripping his guitar on the edge of our bed, singing to my belly rounded with our son. Performances such as today's stroked Simon's ego. That moment only *I* could remember, nearly thirteen years ago, was love. Unfiltered, raw, and potent.

What I'd always dreamed our life would be.

I blinked back the memory and firmed my chin. Jeremiah needed to see his father, and I…well, I had some important details to share with Simon as well.

Simon bowed, his dark hair falling onto his forehead, his hazel eyes bright as he waved to this cheering crowd, signaling the end of his set. He walked off the other side of the stage, still unaware of our presence. I squeezed Jeremiah's hand and began the arduous effort of maneuvering around the large crew who would be setting up for the next group to take the stage—some hip-hop act I wasn't familiar with. Much as I loved music, I was also single parenting and much too exhausted to find time for

1

new musicians I wanted to follow.

"What's the plan, Mom?"

"Find your father and yell surprise. What else would we do, love?"

Jeremiah bit his lip, eyes rounding with anxiety. "You sure he's going to be glad to see us?"

Same refrain, different day. "Of course, my darling. Don't fret. Your father's been busy living his dream. But now it's time to remind him of his best accomplishment." I slung my arm over Jeremiah's shoulder, pulling him closer to my side.

"Dad!" Jeremiah cried, freeing himself from my embrace to break into a run. He flung his arms around Simon's waist. Simon, for his part, recovered after a couple of staggering steps and hugged Jeremiah back, no longer needing to bend over so he could press his cheek to Jeremiah's crown. A pang of disappointment slammed through me—Jeremiah, now twelve, reached Simon's nose. Last time they'd been together, Jeremiah was at least an inch—probably more—shorter.

"Good to see you, bud." He stood to his full height and caught sight of me. "Ella."

His eyes lit up and he smiled, making me ache.

"This is the best Christmas surprise."

"Really, Simon?" I asked, a catch building in my throat as I fingered the papers in my bag. "*That's* how you want to play this?"

Jeremiah glanced between us, his teeth sunk deep into his lower lip to keep it from quivering. "Not here," Jeremiah whispered. His lip began to tremble. "Not now."

But Simon either didn't hear Jeremiah's plea or chose to ignore it. "Play what?" he asked, his brows pulling low over his nose.

The bloody, bloody…twat! I pulled the thick sheaf from the depths of my bag. "The divorce papers you had served to me at *school*? In front of my entire sophomore choral class. Yes, dear, I did receive those. Thank you *so much* for the humiliation."

"Not now," Jeremiah practically wailed.

"What the hell are you talking about, Ella?" Simon's voice was hard. If I hadn't been holding the incriminating documents, I might have paused, considered the look on his face. But, as I watched, his lovely hazel eyes darkened, and he scowled.

He had no right to be upset with me. Not after those pictures. Not after him doing *this* to me.

"Your son wanted to meet his stepmum."

Simon stepped back, affronted. "What has gotten into you? I'm married to you. *Only* you."

"Right. Good to hear straight from your mouth since that's not what we've both read on the internet—not that you'd bothered to call and tell us any of this yourself." I swallowed back the ball of emotion that built in my chest, burning up my throat. He'd promised to love me, forever. And, silly me, I believed him—believed in us—even after pictures came out two months ago: pictures of him cuddling in close to Monique, his publicist. The speculation about our impending divorce skyrocketed, but Simon played blasé, saying the entire situation was overblown and he'd see us soon. Then, two weeks later, came the photo of her *kissing* him.

"Well, then, since you don't want *us*"—I stood up straighter and dropped the papers at my feet—"we'll be off."

"Ella," Simon growled. I'd bet his anger stemmed from the fact Jeremiah was already back at my side, grasping my hand like

3

the lifeline to normalcy it was.

I turned my head back over my shoulder, trying to calm my racing heart. "Oh. And just wanted to let you know your solicitor needs to step up a new monthly stipend for us, seeing as we're expecting another child. Merry Christmas!" I forced as much cheer into the words as I could, knowing I'd never, *ever*, find this time of year happy or magical again. Not since Simon bloody ruined my life and the excitement of the new child we'd been trying to conceive for eight years.

I didn't bother to look back, just continued to clutch Jeremiah's hand in mine as we wended our way back through the growing crowd. Simon called my name again. And once more, I ignored him.

"Did you really have to tell him like that?" Jeremiah asked.

This time, I was the one to bite my lip, hoping it would stem my tears. They spilled over my lashes against my will. "Hadn't planned on it, no."

Jeremiah sighed. "Mason said adults are weird when they divorce."

The painful sting behind my eyes spread to my nose as more tears poured down my cheeks. I stopped my mad march toward the exit and cupped my son's cheeks. "No matter what happens, I love you."

"Ella!" Simon's voice held a note of desperation.

"Bloody *hell*." I did not want to deal with my soon-to-be ex anymore, especially not now that the tears brimmed. Jeremiah's eyes pleaded with mine for a moment before he looked beyond me at what I assumed was his father. Jeremiah's eyes narrowed and his mouth settled into a grim line.

"Time to go, Mom. And I love you, too." He leaned into me, his arm going around my waist.

Right. I shouldn't turn around. No way Jeremiah would say that if it wasn't bad. So, of course, I looked. And nearly fell to my knees. The woman Simon had been photographed with these past few weeks—the reason I made the snarky stepmum comment— plastered herself to his front, her arms wound around his neck, and her tongue shoved way down his throat. Fucking bastard. Couldn't he save that for when his son—when *I*—couldn't see?

I staggered, but Jeremiah stayed firm, unwavering presence at my side. Gulping in needed air, I gripped Jeremiah's hand and let him tow me through the crowd this time. At least the tears stopped.

"Ella!" Simon shouted again. I didn't bother to look back, just raised my left hand and gave him the same finger he'd given me in my work place yesterday. I refused to turn around, refused to talk to him again. He'd made his choice and he could bloody well live with the consequences, including the fact he'd never know the child I now carried.

Somehow, we were at the rental car. I was shaking so hard, I wasn't sure I could drive. But no way I could stay here to further my humiliation. I cursed Simon Dorsey with every word I could think of. Not enough, not *ever* enough, but he'd taken the choice from me—yanked my security from me and decimated the love I still felt for him.

Time to move forward. Into divorcee single motherhood.

Happy bloody Christmas.

CHAPTER TWO
Simon

Those first moments when Ella stood there, before dropping the sheaf of papers—and the bigger bomb of her pregnancy—at my feet, I *thrilled* to see her. She was more beautiful than ever. Even before she spoke, she'd shattered my anger and aggravation at the way we'd left our last few conversations. Sure, I was frustrated she thought I'd cheat on her. She had to know she was all I thought about—her and Jeremiah. As soon as I looked into her eyes, I realized I'd missed her, more than I'd known.

But now…she'd seen me, and the pain in her lovely, light green eyes as she spoke of divorce turned hard when she looked back to find Monique kissing me. No, I didn't kiss her back. I couldn't, not with Jeremiah watching and, more importantly, because I didn't want to.

Monique wasn't my wife.

I clutched at my chest, unsure which was worse—the pain in Ella's eyes or the disappointment and anger in Jeremiah's.

Both. All of it. *What the hell happened just now?*

"Where did she get divorce papers?" I asked.

"You told the lawyer to send them. Remember?"

I mostly certainly did *not* remember. I'd visited his office one time—once—just after Ella and I fought nearly two months ago. Over the pictures of Monique and me in the papers. Monique suggested that visit—her and Gerard—saying I'd be better off without Ella holding me back, causing my emotional distress.

More and more over the past few months, I'd come to realize I could have Ella or I could have my career, but I couldn't balance both. I'd thought giving her up was the smart decision—the best choice for *my* future.

I'd listened. But as soon as I had walked into the office, my stomach tightened. I thought of Ella's laugh. Her sardonic wit. The way she cuddled up against me at night, her hand always wrapped around my arm, hugging it to her.

I'd answered the questions my lawyer asked. But with each response, my heart grew heavier.

"This is wrong," I'd said, standing.

"I have a few more questions, Mr. Dorsey, then we can draw up the papers. Do you have a prenuptial agreement?"

"No." I'd walked around the chair and placed both palms on the glossy conference table. "And I don't plan to sue for divorce. This was a mistake." A really stupid one. "Forget I was ever here."

"But Mr. Dorsey…"

"I said forget it."

"Baby?" Monique touched my cheek, turning my head so I would look down into her bright brown eyes. Model beautiful, thin, and glamorous, Monique didn't do it for me. Not like Ella did. Always had.

"My name's Simon." I stepped back, craning my neck for another glimpse of Ella.

Because, in that moment, I realized something monumental: I didn't just love my wife. I adored her as I had since she trounced me in cricket all those years ago. But, somehow, I'd blown our happiness away with my dream. Worse still, Ella thought I was screwing around on her.

Merry goddamn Christmas to me.

"Where are you going?" Monique called as I broke into a sprint.

No way I was letting Ella leave. Not now that she'd told me she was pregnant. *A baby.* Warmth spread through my chest, my stomach, wrapped around my heart.

A baby. She couldn't be that far along—not with as flat as her tummy was. And…up until the last couple of months, she would have told me as soon as she missed her period—her not-quite-regular cycle. I frowned, remembering what led to those irregularities, not liking where my mind, and probably Ella's, went, when she first discovered her pregnancy. To the miscarriages we'd weathered over the years.

I wondered for how long she's known. How long she's been keeping this from me. But with my travel schedule, and those stupid pictures popping up in the gossip pages, Ella quit trusting me—even with something as important as this new child. And the fear this pregnancy would end, too soon, like the last two.

But a baby…hot damn. I wanted another child with El. With Jeremiah. I wanted to be a family, to spend time with them. To cuddle them all close to my heart. To croon out songs and feel the tiny breaths against my throat.

Monique's long nails dug into my sleeve as she tried to pull me around to face her. "What do you think you're doing?" she asked again, her breath breaking as she struggled to keep up.

I shook off her hand. "Going to *my wife*."

I jogged forward, craning my neck. There. Her brown hair glinted in the wintry sun, flashing with bits of gold brought out by the sun's rays. They were at the entrance. Jeremiah seemed to be holding up much of Ella's sleight weight. Was she sick? She'd been so ill with Jeremiah, barely gaining enough for the baby.

"Ella!" I shouted.

She didn't turn back, just saluted me with her middle finger. Jeremiah did, though, and the look on his face caused me to stumble to a stop. He pulled Ella closer to his side and quickened his pace, putting as much distance between us as he could.

My son hated me.

"You don't have a wife," Monique said from my side. "I was there when you visited your lawyer. You remember why, baby?" Monique crooned, running her palm up my arm. "She's holding back your career. She didn't want you to add to your touring schedule. She's keeping you from *real* fame and respect."

Monique spoke in a soft, soothing voice—a siren whose words caused earthquakes and destruction. She wrapped her arms around mine and pulled my biceps to her breasts, trying to ensnare me further into her web of darkness.

"That means *we* can get married. Start our own family if you want." I turned toward her in time to see her smile. "I'd love to have a baby with you, Simon." Her eyes, before her lashes dropped into a seductive, bedroom pose, flashed with greed.

She wanted a child with me to secure her place in my life—and bank account. Not because she loved me. Or even liked me.

I'd fallen for Monique's spiel before—that's how I ended up considering the possibility of leaving my wife. Monique stroked my pride—such a beautiful woman showing interest in me—but that interest went only as far as my ability to stay on the Billboard's Top 200 list.

With slow precision, I pulled my arms from hers. I stepped back so we were a good five feet apart. "Don't ever come near me again."

Her mouth dropped open and her eyes flashed with vindictive

outrage. "I'm your publicist!"

"Not anymore. You're fired. My guess is you had something to do with those papers Ella had served to her at her school."

My chest rose and fell. *At her school.* Ella wasn't just hurt, she must be mortified. That she could ever think I'd do something like that to her made my ears burn with anger.

Monique narrowed her eyes before spinning on her heel to stomp away. Something told me I wasn't going to like Monique's next move any better than Ella's.

Catching the glare of a camera lens, I tucked my hands into my pockets and headed over to the paparazzi, hoping to ask one of them for the photographic proof of Monique's attempt to further disrupt my relationship with my family.

My need to protect Ella's feelings reared up, shocking me with its intensity. I'd thought of her before Jeremiah—not my normal modus operandi these past few months. When had I stopped thinking about Ella? *Why* had I quit?

Because as my fame increased, her enthusiasm tanked, which hurt my pride, but, more, my feelings. I felt like she didn't want me to achieve the success my brother-in-law Asher had. Like she didn't think I was worthy of the adulation.

I rubbed my hand across the back of my neck, annoyed when the pap ran off. Not surprising, but now I had a new conundrum: How to get those pictures when I didn't have anyone on my team with connections to the media?

I needed to call Ella. Futile though it would be. Ella might look like a sweet English sprite, but the woman held a grudge better than anyone I'd ever met. She said it was because she was a Scorpio. Whatever the hell one had to do with the other.

I stooped down and grabbed the papers Ella had dropped at my feet.

Ella. So many questions circled through my head. Did she know the sex of the baby? Most important in my mind was the question of whether she and the baby were healthy. Did the baby have Huntington's, the disease that killed my brother and father?

I pulled myself up into my trailer. Gerard stood in the small kitchen, nibbling at his fingernails.

"Tell me, Gerard. How did Ella get these?" I slammed the papers onto the counter as I glared at my paunchy manager. He blanched and bit harder at his next nail.

"I-I don't know. This is *not* going to go over well with the label."

Ella's shattered eyes popped to mind, followed by Jeremiah's disgusted sneer. I grabbed the papers and moved to the living area and settled into one of the arm chairs.

I should have taken Asher up on his suggestion to chat with him about fame. But, once again, I'd let my pride stand in front of my intelligence...and ignorance. Now Ella and Jeremiah were paying the full price, thinking I no longer wanted them.

That was a deadshot between the eyes. One I didn't know how to fix—if I could ever fix it.

My fingers gripped the edges of the papers hard enough for multiple pieces to slice into the pad of my thumb. I winced but didn't relinquish my hold, even knowing the grip on my guitar strings tomorrow would be weak and painful.

"I'm worried about my family. Not the label's response."

"Well, you better care about their response. They can break your career, Simon."

I blew out a breath, my eyes flicking to the door where Gerard headed. Where was he going? Probably cooking up something nefarious with Monique. I'd sort him in a minute. Time to deal with the most pressing problem first.

I rotated my head on my neck, trying to ease the tension there. When that didn't help, I picked up my phone and dialed Asher's number.

"Lia's so pissed at you," he said in lieu of greeting.

"If it makes you feel any better, I'm pretty pissed, too."

"Doesn't. Ella's beat herself up over your divorce—Lia was over there the night you sent the papers. Who drops shit like that? Oh, and Mason said Jeremiah cried in the school bathroom on Friday."

I clenched my free hand tight, fighting the urge to punch something. "Shit. I fired Monique because she kissed me in front of Jeremiah and Ella."

"Considering the world thinks you're screwing her, Lia and I included, I don't see why you'd get upset about a kiss."

I slammed my fist against the table. "I'm *not* having an affair."

"Just divorcing your pregnant wife of fifteen years so you *can* screw around. Nice."

"You got a divorce," I bit out.

"Sure did." Asher's voice turned cheerful. "Best decision I ever made. Well, except pursuing Dahlia. That was really my best move ever. Should have done it nineteen years earlier and then she wouldn't be related to you. Even if it is only by marriage."

"I need a new manager and PR pro," I yelled over the top of Asher's next sentence. The man was intentionally pissing me off.

"Then find one."

"You know people."

"Thought I knew you, too," he shot back.

I dropped my head into my hands. "I don't plan on divorcing Ella. I never did. I didn't even know she was going to be served papers."

"What?" His voice turned soft. Deadly.

"That's what I've been trying to tell you! I never asked my lawyer to send Ella divorce papers."

"There had to be something on file—"

"Look, I'm pretty sure pictures of Monique kissing me are about to hit a lot of sites, and that's going to hurt Ella and Jeremiah more. Can you help me out? Who can I call to work on this? Asher, Ella's pregnant. You weren't around for the last one." I swallowed down the panic building in my throat. "She was so sick. She's going to need me. Now. I have to figure out what went wrong and do damage control so I don't lose my wife."

I dropped my head in my hands and heaved a breath.

"I love her. Shit. Fuck. I love Ella. She can't think I did this. She can't…"

"I'll see what I can do with the PR personnel. But you better get to the source of the problem," Asher said.

"Besides the constant touring? Jeremiah didn't want to leave his friends and Ella didn't want to quit her job. She loves her students and Jeremiah's a social kid. There's no way I could ask them to join my entourage at the expense of their happiness."

"Did you ever *ask*? Did you ever *give* Ella that choice?"

I blew out a shocked breath. "No." I blinked in rapid succession. "No, I never asked Ella if she wanted to come with me."

"Seems to me you did bring some of this on yourself." Asher

grunted. "Lia heard all this. She's making puppy dog eyes. I'll make some calls. For her. For Ella. Get your shit together, man."

CHAPTER THREE
Ella

Flying to Heathrow this go-round proved the worst trip ever—partly because Atlanta's airport overflowed with travelers, creating bottlenecks and sheer difficulty to navigate.

Jeremiah's sullen silence worsened my mood. And all those inconveniences compounded with recurring nausea. Up until tonight, I experienced no symptoms with this pregnancy. I'd been so excited about this child—a girl, I'd found out the day before Simon dropped his bombshell of divorce on my cluttered oak desk.

I snorted, pulling the blanket to my chin as I thought back to how I'd planned my surprise—one of the benefits of having to take the prenatal test called CVS last week was that I managed to find out my baby's gender—not much earlier than I would have with the second regular sonogram I'd had this week so that I'd have a picture to give to Simon. The tangible proof of what our love together produced.

But the last few months, with all the pictures and speculation about Simon flying around, proved difficult for us both, causing our relationship to pull taut—to the breaking point, apparently. The stress of those weeks after the first picture came out, and Simon's subsequent brush-off, made me assume my irregular cycle was due to stress. I might not have known I was pregnant even now if I hadn't been scheduled to see my OB/GYN for my annual exam two weeks ago. She'd whisked me straight into the CVS testing and brought me back for a sonogram just days later, her happy smile telling me as much as her words.

This baby—finally—was healthy. I still couldn't believe how

15

far along I was.

That's why I'd purchased the tickets to Atlanta, and I'd found the cutest, pink cashmere infant dress and bonnet—that was priced at a ridiculous amount for the mere weeks the baby would wear it—and I'd bought the darling outfit, planning to wrap it up with the sonogram for Simon's main present.

The gift lay at the bottom of my large roll-on, no doubt crushed by my winter boots and thick cable-knit sweaters necessary for the trip to my parent's getaway in Bath. Not unlike my dreams for bringing my family back together.

Unable to partake in a glass of wine to calm my raging emotions and help me relax, I idly ran my hand over Jeremiah's thick, dark hair, smoothing the many cowlicks. He looked so much like Simon. Each time I turned, saw the back of his dark head, the set of his shoulders, my heart ached for the destruction of my marriage I'd never seen coming.

Sure, Simon traveled often, but that was for logistical reasons. I had a job; Jeremiah had school and soccer, friends and play dates. We'd planned to spend Christmas together at my parents' house, take a trip to Hawaii for spring break—which coincided with our fifteenth wedding anniversary. Simon even curtailed some of his touring options next summer so that Jeremiah and I could spend as much time with him as possible.

In the interim, single parenting remained difficult, and, no, I didn't appreciate the constancy of Simon's travel schedule. But up until last week, I hadn't worried about Simon leaving me.

More fool I.

I shifted, trying to get more comfortable. Trying, without success, to ease the burning ache in my stomach and the roiling, noxious poison of my heartache.

Jeremiah lifted his head and blinked at me, his eyes bleary. Whatever he saw in my face made him sit up and grab my hand. He'd never been much of a cuddler, always a robust ball of energy.

"We're going to be okay, Mom. Really. I talked with Mason about this."

I closed my gritty eyes with a wince. "You'd said."

"Try not to worry. I heard Aunt Lia say it's not good for you or the baby."

I smiled at Jeremiah's earnest tone. "She said stress isn't good for me or the baby?" Couldn't get much more stressful than turning thirty-six and finding oneself pregnant and alone.

"Aunt Lia said you're not alone."

I squeezed his fingers for a moment, searching for the right words to say to my child. I wasn't sure what those words were, though. "Oh, love, I'm not. I have you, and your aunt and Asher and your grandparents. As you said, we'll be fine."

Jeremiah turned toward me, his beautiful hazel eyes, Simon's eyes, solemn. "I'll make sure of it."

This time I had to look away so my son wouldn't see the tears I refused to shed. Simon had said just that to me when we found out I was pregnant with Jeremiah.

And even he changed his tune.

———◆———

My parents met us just outside customs, much to my disgruntlement. I'd wanted time to use the loo and wash the fatigue and worry from my face. My mum clucked as she drew me in for a hug.

"There, now. Oh, poppet. We're here for you, my darling."

I squeezed my eyes together tight as I cuddled into my marshmallow-soft mum. "It's worse than I thought."

My mother extricated herself from my embrace and clasped my cheeks between her soft, plump hands.

"Don't add to the worry. We'll help you see this through," she said, her voice turning brisk.

I hated to cry, preferring always to put forth a strong, capable front. I sucked in a deep breath, grateful for the moment to gather my jagged emotions.

"So, the good news is you had the test, and it came back negative. That's worth celebrating." My father's jovial words struck me, each an emotional blow, but I put up a brave front.

"Right. Yes. Brilliant to know our gel won't develop Huntington's."

While I was ecstatic to not have to worry about my new child in that regard, I still couldn't wrap my head around the fact I was about to become a divorcée.

"Simon's seeing someone," I blurted out. "She's younger than me by a good five years."

"He *kissed* her at that concert. In *front* of us," Jeremiah said, shouldering his duffel bag, his freckled cheeks suffused in angry red color.

"Off to the car with you," my father said, his eyes wide.

Yeah, this was going to be the merriest of Christmases. My mother grabbed another of our bags and wrapped her arm around my waist, cinching me tight to her side. "We've a lovely fresh blanket of snow. And it's perfect hot cocoa weather."

Jeremiah continued to scowl but at least he didn't say

anything further about his father.

———◆———

I turned on my phone and opened my laptop upon arrival to my parents' house to see the picture of Monique—Simon's publicist who was supposed to keep him out of bad press for Pete's sake!—and nearly three thousand emails. I shut down both and handed them over to my mother for safekeeping.

"I can't deal with the concern from Lia and Briar and my friends any better than I can the request for a statement."

Mum wiped her flour-covered hands on her apron and took both devices from me in a ginger grip as if she expected them to blow up in her face.

"What if Simon calls?" she asked after taking my laptop to my father's small study.

"It's off. It'll go to voice mail."

"But what if he needs to talk to you?"

"Then feel free to turn on my phone and tell him to stuff it," I said.

"Ella." Her voice held the same shrill displeasure as when I colored a mustache on my third-grade teacher's picture. "I raised you better than that."

"You raised me to honor my vows, too." I stood, grabbing the wooden back of the chair for support until the encroaching darkness passed. Mum stepped nearer, concern etching into her cheeks. I waved her off. "Is Jeremiah at the park ice-skating with Dad?"

"Yes. Your father said they'd be another hour, maybe more. They'll be back in time for lunch."

"Right. I'll meet them down there. I need some fresh air."

"You sure you don't want to rest? Might do you and the nipper some good."

I slid my arms into my thick down-filled coat. "Too restless. I'll only be gone a bit."

"Take your mobile." Mum shoved the hated device back at me. When I made no move to take it, she dropped it into my coat pocket. "I won't have you leaving unless I have a way to contact you."

I pulled the phone from my pocket and made sure it was switched to silent. No way I was going increase my mental strain on each new call, text, or email.

I'd marched halfway to the park before the fatigue and overwhelming sadness crashed over me. Slowing my pace to meander, I settled on a bench at the edge of the greenspace, needing a moment to collect my thoughts and slow my breathing before meeting up with my son. Jeremiah would look to me for strength, to help guide him through this scary new world we'd been thrust into.

Problem was, I didn't have a good plan to attack this alien, Simon-free world.

"Ella Parker?"

I lifted my head, brow furled against the blinding light of late-morning sun on snow. "Yes? Oh, hello Philip. Nice to see you."

"Pleasure's all mine," he said, slipping onto the bench next to me, close enough for our thighs to brush. He leaned in farther and, in a panic, I realized he planned to hug me. I patted his back with perfunctory politeness, willing him to release me from his grip.

"Ella Parker! Blimey. I thought you were in America."

"I was. Am, I guess. I live in Seattle. And it's Dorsey. Ella Dorsey. Or, rather, was." I swallowed down that damn vicious lump of emotion. "I'm in process of divorcing my husband."

"Are you, now? That's a right shame. For him and you."

"More so for me. He's got a new love." My smile was somewhere between watery and full of bite.

"Terribly rough on you, I'd bet. Though I'm still buggered to see you at all. I've thought of you, Ella." He settled back against the wood slats, hands tucked between his parted knees.

My first love—that I'd blown—sitting on a bench in a park in Bath as I agonized over my current love who'd practically admitted to an affair just yesterday. Life wasn't kind, but she sure had a wicked sense of humor.

"I'm not much for company," I said on a sigh. "I came to collect my son."

"How old is he?"

"Twelve."

"And you live in Seattle?"

"We do. Did." I clutched at the edges of my coat, willing my world to right. "I'm not sure what we'll do now." My voice broke off to naught more than a whisper.

Philip's warm brown eyes caught my gaze and held it. "If you decide to stay 'round here, I'd be chuffed to help."

I stared at him, helpless to stem the flow of my emotions any more than I knew how to answer him. He raised his hand and tucked a lose strand of my hair back into my white knit cap. "You're as beautiful as I remembered."

"I'm pregnant," I blurted out.

His eyes hardened, mimicking the set of his jaw. "And your

husband *left* you?"

I gulped, dipping my head in affirmation as my eyes fell to my wool-lined boots. Philip pulled me into another hug, and this one I melted into, needing the reassurance of another person. The truths were ugly, and bottom line was I hated the mess I'd made of my life.

"Ah, Ella. I hate to see you sad."

"He didn't know. Unexpected. Anyway, I should…I should go. Jeremiah's already struggling, thanks to Simon's bombshell. I don't want him to be more upset because he caught me cuddling a strange man in the park."

"Am I a stranger, Ella?"

"You're…no, Philip." I sniffled but managed a smile. "No. You are a wonderful person."

His smile brightened his face. "Are you staying at your parents' house?"

I nodded, my brows puckered.

He squeezed my mitten hand. "I'll call on you tomorrow."

"Oh, that's not—"

He stood, towering over me. "I'll see you tomorrow, Ella. I'm glad to have run into you."

He started to walk away, but that damn curiosity that ate at Jeremiah came from me. "Wait! What are you doing here in Bath?"

He turned back, his brown hair fluffed by the soft breeze. "I'm going to a meeting."

"Entrepreneurship worked well for you, I hope." I smiled. It was tremulous but real. It grew as I saw Jeremiah running along the path toward me.

"Quite well. I'll talk to you more tomorrow. I'm a bit late."

He turned and skirted Jeremiah, who barreled around him and into my arms. Philip turned back to see me hugging my son, then with a slight smile and a dip of his chin, he disappeared into a growing throng of midday walkers.

"Who was that?" Jeremiah asked.

"An old friend. I knew Philip in school."

"Oh."

My father trotted up, puffing from exertion, his cheeks rosier even than Jeremiah's. "That Philip Wagner?"

I nodded.

"Nice chap. Done quite well for himself, I heard. In those apps you kids favor." He tickled Jeremiah's neck, making the boy giggle and swat at his hand.

"He made you smile."

My eyes rose to Jeremiah's, but his lacked the accusation I anticipated. Instead, Jeremiah's eyes turned soft. My heart pounded again.

Was this my life? My child comforting me, worrying over me. Oh, no. That would never do.

"We're old friends. That's all."

And it was—Philip and I spoke occasionally, still friendly, when I met Simon. But I hadn't given my old love more than a second thought as I followed Simon back to Seattle and built my life there, with him.

"Race you home!" Jeremiah called, turning to take off down the path. I breathed a sigh of relief at Jeremiah's exuberance. My rambunctious child remained under the new maturity the past week forced upon him.

My father wrapped his arm over my shoulder, our pace much

more sedate than Jeremiah's breakneck sprint.

"Always did like that boy."

"Jeremiah? I should hope so."

Dad squeezed my shoulder, a comforting reminder of his presence. Peppermint and cool winter air filled my nostrils, easing the tension in my aching neck.

"No, love. Philip. Smart young man. Good head on his shoulders. English to the bone."

"I'm not looking for anything, Dad."

"Never said a word that you were. Just commenting on the nice young man who was here to offer you his broad shoulder to rest your tired head on."

I stopped walking, aware that Jeremiah was waiting for us at the corner, tapping his foot and fidgeting.

"You don't like Simon?" I asked. Surprise built in my chest, spread outward and into my tightening neck muscles.

"I don't like that he's made you sad." Dad tapped his finger to my chin. "I don't like the look in your eyes today. He took your fire, Ella."

I tipped my chin down. "I didn't ever love Philip like I love Simon."

Dad sighed and a white puff of air swirled around our heads.

"You have a great big heart and a lovely, independent spirit. Just the type of daughter I'd always wished for." He tipped my chin up, pinching it. "Now, though, you're hurt and scared, and it makes this father worry. You deserve every happiness, love. Every single one." He pressed a kiss to my forehead and then ushered me toward Jeremiah. I walked back toward my folks' cottage, lost in thought.

CHAPTER FOUR
Simon

I scrubbed my hands over my face, but staring at the picture of Ella snuggled in the arms of her ex-boyfriend didn't make the image—nor my scowl—disappear. If she didn't look so shocked in the first and despondent in the second, I'd…what?

I'd sent her divorce papers. Well…the email came from my account. I'd ferreted that bit out when I called my lawyer earlier, not long after my call to Asher. His secretary forwarded me the original email dated two weeks prior.

I dropped my head into my hands with a groan. What a cluster.

If Ella was tearing up the sheets with Philip right now, it wasn't like I could be angry at her.

Except I was. And jealous. Soul-eating, trailer-wrecking jealous. And I sat on the wrong continent, another show tonight with four more planned over the next seven days.

Asher had warned me not to get caught up in the churn, to manage my schedule and my time so that I didn't end up right *here*, in this predicament. Alone the week before Christmas, and so goddamn lonely I couldn't draw a full breath.

"You need to put out a statement." Gerard's blunt finger tapped my laptop's screen. Didn't matter how many times I asked him not to touch the screen, he grimed the glass with whatever nasty lived on his fingertip. I'd wipe it again later.

"I fired Monique, remember? *You'll* have to put out a statement."

"I don't understand why you did that. She's great at this stuff."

I turned in my chair, forcing Gerard back two full paces,

enough to give me some space. The whole breathing-down-the-back-of-my-neck thing didn't work for me. "She called me baby."

"She calls all her clients baby."

"She kissed me in front of Ella."

Gerard's eyes widened as his lips formed an O.

"And she intimated that *you* wanted me to be with her. Which reminds me that you were the one who suggested, all so casually, that maybe Ella was holding me back—which Monique latched on to awful quick. You said maybe Ella was the reason I wasn't doing more shows and festivals, making us more money."

"I never once suggested you divorce your wife, Simon," Gerard said, his voice as stiff as his neck.

"Didn't you?"

He drew himself up to his full, unimpressive height of five-nine. "You went to visit the lawyer all on your own."

I opened my mouth, only to slam it shut again. We stared at each other until Gerard brought his hand to his mouth, once against gnawing at his nails.

"So, do you like Ella?"

"Hell, no! She has you wrapped around her finger. You do whatever she wants you to even if it's an off-hand text. Look at the three-week hiatus you took last year just as your career was kicking into overdrive. Took us another three months to get back that momentum. And we lost who knows how many hundreds of thousands in revenue because of that stupid decision."

I snorted. "Wrapped around her finger? That can't be true since *she's* in England and *I'm* here with a stack of legalese that claims we're unattaching. All because of an email sent from my account—that I didn't send."

Gerard lowered his hands and placed them on his hips. "I don't like you unhappy. Bad for performances. You stunk last night, and half the crowd disbursed before you finished your set. Don't give me shit about two performances in one day. Do you have any idea how bad that is for future sales?"

Gerard was such an ass. I had to fix my situation with Ella before Philip Wagner shacked up with *my wife*. Quick. Especially now that the media was hot on Ella's trail. She *hated* the cameras in her face and the constant cattiness of comments about what she wore.

For Ella, success, in the form of us being able to pay off our house and buy her a new car—the first she'd ever owned—was fabulous but *fame, recognition,* they were a burden. An albatross around my neck that had yoked her in, too.

I'd never really considered it as such before, but Ella's point had been proven during the past twenty-four hours: this scrutiny, the baited breath with which the world seemed to be hanging on my next move, sucked. And I dragged Ella into it.

Monique must have called all her media contacts yesterday after I fired her. She must have fed them the story of my break-up, complete with the photos of everything from Monique's kiss to Ella's bird salute.

"Get me out of these next shows." I shoved back farther, catching Gerard's foot and causing him to yelp in pain. Better than an argument. I slammed my laptop shut.

"I can't…This is career suicide!" Gerard sputtered.

"That's better than losing my wife and kid."

"You don't mean that. Your son will come around. You're his famous, cool dad. All you have to do is…I don't know…take him

27

somewhere he wants to go. Voila! World's best dad."

My brows shot up. "And Ella?"

Gerard gnawed on his ring finger. "Well. I mean. She's probably going to leave you anyway. Now."

And the weight I'd been carrying crashed against my shoulders with enough force to cause me to stagger.

"How did I let this get so far out of hand?"

I glanced around. I didn't have many people on staff—I wasn't a big name like Asher or Hayden. But I wasn't willing to stick with people who'd lied and cheated, maybe worse, to get their claws deeper into my earnings.

"Clive!" He was my head of—and only—security. I waited for the large ex-biker to stroll over, hands in pockets, tattoos bulging on his thick biceps. "Did you have anything to do with Monique and Gerard conniving to split me and Ella up?"

"Your cute pixie wife?" Clive's voice was deep, his words slow. "Nah, man. I like the little Brit."

I turned back to Gerard, who was nibbling at his nails faster than usual. "First off, Merry Christmas." I pulled out an envelope I'd intended to give Gerard after the performance tomorrow. A large thank-you for building my career and helping me reach this pinnacle of success.

He took it, his expression changing from fearful to confused.

"You've helped me out these past few years, worked your tail off for me. Thanks for all that." Gerard's thin lips started to curve up, his eyes began to gleam. I took a deep breath and said the words, "You're fired."

"What?" His squeal reminded me of the greased pigs Jeremiah and I saw at the rodeo a couple of years ago. Before all this craziness hit.

"You just said I helped you. You can't fire me."

"Already did." I turned to Clive. "Escort him out of the trailer and off the fairgrounds, please."

Clive dipped his head and grasped Gerard's upper arm. The smaller, older man continued to squawk and flail, but Clive's grip was firm, and I didn't doubt Gerard would be off-premises within minutes.

"Oh, wait!" I called. Gerard turned back, a look of triumph on his face, but it quickly turned to defeat when I pulled off his lanyard that held his credentials to get in the back-stage area. "Please make sure security knows he's off all my lists. Monique, too. I don't want to see that woman either."

"Will do," Clive rumbled.

"Thanks," I said.

I opened my laptop and dug through the emails until I found the one to Jon Singer, the record label exec who'd signed me a year and a half ago. After explaining my wife was pregnant and ill—the last bit patently false, but I didn't have scruples left at this point—I signed off my email and started looking at flights to London.

I slammed my head forward on my desk. My email pinged and I grabbed my phone, heart fluttering with the hope it was Ella. But no…this was from Jon, telling me to take care of my family. That if I needed any support, my contact was Angelica Gatlin.

I called the number he gave.

"Angelica." Her voice was sunny, bright, but the words clipped.

"This is Simon Dorsey."

"Yes. Seems you have a PR issue, Mr. Dorsey."

I considered it more of a life one. "I fired Monique. I need a new publicist. And to get out of my upcoming schedule. And to find out who hacked my email and sent a message to my lawyer. And…"

"We have emails from you, responding to all our questions over the past few months. I'll forward them to you. Based on your original note, it seems you aren't aware of the number of correspondences."

'I'm not."

"The emails are on their way. Do you need me to help you make any travel plans? I'm assuming, based on the email from Jon, you're going to see your wife in England."

"Yeah." I blew out a breath. "I'll make those. Just…can you help with the media?"

"Jon wants me on this crisis until it's completed. I'll fly out to England as soon as I work through the immediate issues."

"Er, well, thanks, Ms. Gatlin."

"Call me Angelica. And for the record, I'm not a fan of Monique."

A few more emails popped into my inbox. I squinted at the tiny headers. All about my contract and touring.

I opened them, my stomach aching more with each message.

I'd given Gerard access to my email—seemed smart at the time so that he could respond to important messages more quickly than I'd have been able to.

I created a new password for my email, then for all my social media accounts, and even my phone. Paranoid? Maybe. But I wasn't taking any chances. Not after yesterday's debacle.

I'd read the rest of the messages later—on the plane.

I rubbed the palms of my hands over my gritty eyes. I picked up my phone and dialed Ella's phone number. Straight to voice mail. Of course. No way I'd get in touch with her unless I stood in the same room with her.

"Ella," I started. I blew out a breath. "We need to talk. I don't know what happened. Please call me."

She wouldn't. Ella was stubborn—and right now, hurt. She probably deleted any and all messages I sent.

With a few clicks on the website, I booked a flight. The only way to work this out—work this through—was in person. As quickly as possible.

My plane left in three hours.

I jumped from my chair and pulled out my suitcase.

CHAPTER FIVE
Ella

Philip arrived next morning around 10:00 a.m., his bespoke suit covered in a dark charcoal cashmere coat that enhanced his eyes and pointed to his wealth and status—in that typical understated British way I missed. The United States was many things, but understated was not top of list. Philip handed me a posy of pink and purple sweet peas that I lifted to my nose, inhaling their fragrance with a small hum of pleasure.

"Thank you." I raised my tired, gritty eyes to his. "I adore sweet peas."

"I remember." He removed his coat and settled it onto the sofa next to him. I'd taken the overstuffed club chair—a mistake with my growing belly, but also strategic. I didn't want Jeremiah to see me cozying up next to another man. Not after Simon's kiss with Monique yesterday. Keeping Jeremiah front in my mind wasn't difficult. Like me, his world, his safety, was smashed to bits this week.

Speaking of, my son barreled into the room, brows pulled low to glower at Philip.

"You were with my mom yesterday."

Philip stood and offered his hand. "I was."

Jeremiah scowled, but his innate good manners overcame his frustration and he shook Philip's hand.

"What do you want with my mom?" Jeremiah asked, pulling himself up so he met Philip's eyes directly.

Philip's lips quirked up in a hint of a smile as he took stock of my son.

"Jeremiah," I said on a sigh.

"Don't worry El-Bel." My cheeks reddened at the endearment, one I hadn't heard since Philip went off to uni and I stayed home to finish Year Twelve. "He's just looking out for you." He settled himself back on the stiff sofa cushion and patted the seat beside him. "I'm your mum's friend, first and foremost." He raised his eyebrow, waiting for me to deny the connection we used to share.

Jeremiah refused the offer of a seat and instead crossed his arms over his chest. "But you like her. Gramps said you to use to go out."

"I dated Philip about twenty years ago, darling." No reason to beat around the bush.

"Your mother was my first love." Philip's smile turned sad. "My only love outside my work, really."

"Philip, I don't—"

"But, you see, she's smart, your mother. And she knew, even at seventeen, I wasn't ever going to be the man she needed."

Oh. My heart ached at his words. For a year and a half, Philip was my everything.

"You, like, want to get with her now or something?"

Jeremiah's hands fisted, and Philip, acting the fool, patted his balled-up hands. "Not at all."

I jerked, surprised but the surety in Philip's voice.

"Your mother's coming out of a relationship with your father. One, I daresay, took her by surprise and hurt her."

Jeremiah nodded, his eyes losing some of the shuttered defensiveness I hated. "Then what *do* you want?"

Always curious. But now, suspicious, too. I closed my eyes, too weary of the constant ache in my heart to correct Jeremiah's manners.

"What I want isn't the question. Your mother needs people who care for her. I'm one of those people, same as you."

Philip's words should have filled me with pleasure, but they didn't. Dread ate at the edges of my mind, overwhelming me. Simon filed for divorce. We'd had no separation. He just…left me because I no longer fit his life.

I wasn't ready for this. Any of it.

I bowed my head, once again refusing to let the tears build or fall.

Jeremiah sucked in a big breath that caused a slight whistle when it passed his teeth. "Well, that's okay, I guess. If you just want to be friends. Mom could use one of those while we're here. But don't go hurting her feelings or anything. She's pregnant and needs to chill out."

I stifled a laugh as I raised my head. "Let me guess—Briar?"

"Yeah, Aunt Briar said babies take up lots more space in your head and heart than in your body."

"Smart lady, your aunt," Philip said with a smile in his voice.

"Yeah, she's okay," Jeremiah said with a shrug. "You sure you don't want to date my mom? Or kiss her?" Jeremiah practically growled those last words.

Philip leaned in closer, his eyes twinkling. "Well, who wouldn't want to kiss her? She's very pretty. But I won't." Philip raised his hands, palms up in a gesture of supplication. "Kinsmen's promise."

"What's that?" Jeremiah asked, back to being suspicious.

"I promise on my father's grave I shan't kiss you mother or do anything else you could construe as romantic or inappropriate."

Jeremiah studied Philip for a long moment. "All right. See that you don't." He turned to me, his expression filled with concern, looking so much like his father; I couldn't stop the lump forming in my throat. Why did I keep having this reaction? No one died. My son glowed with health and energy, my baby lay safe in my womb. Jeremiah wrapped his arm around my shoulder in a gentle gesture, completely at odds with his typical exuberance, and kissed my cheek.

"Gramps, Gran, and I are going to go get the tree."

"Oh! I'll go, too."

Jeremiah's face morphed into the same stern lines Simon's did when he was displeased with me. "You will not. Gran wants you to stay here and rest." When I opened my mouth to argue, he said, "Please, Mom."

I snapped my jaw shut and smiled, cupping his cheek. "I like the fluffy ones."

Jeremiah rolled his eyes. "Yeah, yeah. Tall and fluffed. I know the drill." Then, his eyes welled with tears and his lip quivered. "That's…that's what we always get. Can we…"

"Get something different?" I asked, my hand now trembling against his cheek. I brought him forward into my full embrace, rocking him gently. "Whatever you want, my love."

Jeremiah clutched my back, his fingertips digging into my skin through my thick sweater.

"Love you, my precious boy."

He nodded, his nose pressed into my neck. "Love you, too, Mom." He stood with a huff, swiping at his eyes. "'Kay. Well, we're off."

I startled. "Right now?"

35

"Yeah. Gran and Gramps are in the car. I just"—he glanced over at Philip—"I wanted to say bye."

I nodded, a bit dazed. "Enjoy."

Jeremiah walked from the room, and I mourned the lack of his normal scamper.

"I read about you online. I didn't realize the divorce was so new."

"Found out five days ago," I said as I turned back to Philip, trying to compose my face into some semblance of listening, but my mind spun back to our first Christmas with Jeremiah. I would never celebrate our daughter's firsts with Simon. Would I even have the kids next Christmas? My stomach churned as I considered the life of a broken family, splitting time betwixt homes, my children forced to accommodate different traditions.

Simon, why did you do this to us?

CHAPTER SIX
Simon

The back door was unlatched, just as it always had been. With the small Audi out of the driveway, I assumed the family must be picking out a Christmas tree—one of my favorite traditions they practiced even in Seattle.

I let myself in through the back door, surprised by the butter and crumbs on the counters and plates still on the table. My mother-in-law's fastidiousness overruled any family outing. My breath caught and held as I wondered if something happened to Ella.

I darted down the back hallway toward the front of the house. Nothing.

No one at all.

The tree stood in the corner of the room, just where it always had. I sighed in relief, thankful for the continuity. But, the tree itself was different. Tall, thin. Not at all the type Ella typically fell in love with. I walked closer, my heart thumping hard in my chest. The ornaments were new, shiny. Scratch-free and in gold and white, colors we'd never used before on a tree here or at our house in Seattle.

I crouched down, grimacing as I noticed the few presents under the tree. Shoved to the very back, deep under the needles, was a bag with my name on it in Ella's writing. My palms sweated and my heart rate ratcheted, but I managed to tug the bag forward from between the thick needles. I weighed my options.

She must have bought this in Seattle—I knew the name of the boutique; one of the upscale baby stores Ella drooled over each time we walked past it. Did she get it before I sent her the divorce papers? Best guess was yes Ella planned, prepared.

My heart ached because the divorce would have shocked her as much as it hurt—she had no time to consider alternatives or plan for anything. Just…bam! All those years together, over.

Which meant she was very, very angry.

Dammit. I couldn't wait to ask.

I pulled out the tissue paper and gasped, hand hovering over the pink baby bonnet in the bag. On top of that lay a picture. A three-dimensional one that I'd seen with other's children but not with Jeremiah. He was too old for this 3-D technology.

Already, I could see Ella's triangle chin. Her sweet bow mouth.

I ran my fingertips over the photo, my breath caught in my cest. A girl. We were having a girl.

Footsteps pounded up the front walk, along with Jeremiah's laughter. The front door burst open before I managed to stuff the picture back into the bag.

Jeremiah's laugh ended midgasp, his eyes hardening as they landed on me.

"What are you doing here?" he demanded.

Dave and Marsha entered behind, eyes widening when they saw me, but my gaze settled on Ella, who stood behind her parents. Next to Philip.

I gripped the handle of the bag and rocked back on my heels, unsure what to do next.

"What the hell is going on here?" I growled, eyes locked on Philip's hand, which was resting on Ella's shoulder.

"Oh, like you get to ask that question," Jeremiah sneered.

My gaze switched back to my son.

"Jeremiah." My voice held a warning note.

For the first time ever, my son ignored me as he swaggered closer, eyes narrowing. "What? You're going to *ground* me? News flash. I live with Mom now, and that means *not with you*!"

His shoulder slammed into my arm as he strode past me, feet slapping up the steps toward his room. Moments later, the door crashed closed, followed moments later by the thud of a picture falling of the wall and the biting sound of breaking glass.

"Oh, dear." Marsha put her hands to her rosy cheeks, eyes wide. "I better see what's fallen." She and Dave hurried into the house, but not until Dave shot me a look typically reserved for dog shit on a shoe.

I gripped the bag's handles tighter, my shoulders tensing as I brought my eyes back around to Ella, who hovered in the doorway.

Philip kept a solicitous hand on her elbow. "Want me to stay?" he murmured, not bothering to look at me. As if I wasn't important enough to concern himself about. His eyes never wavered from Ella's face, though her eyes darted from mine to Philip's and back. Her cheeks lost the bright spots of color the cold air and exercise had brought about moments before.

"No. But thank you. For the hot cocoa, too."

His smile remained warm, almost intimate.

The asshole was still in love with her. And he'd been with her this week while I…wasn't.

"I'd like to talk with *my wife*," I said.

Philip's wry glance landed on me for the first time. "Huh. You're right. He doesn't like to share. Must have been the photos of us together, El Bel."

My shoulders tightened further and my jaw clamped rigid when he leaned down and pressed a kiss to her pale cheek.

"I'll ring you later."

Ella nodded, her eyes still bouncing back and forth between us. Philip leaned in and whispered something in her ear. Her gaze snapped back to his and she nodded, her mouth settled in a solemn line.

I stepped forward, unwilling to watch this…this…man touch Ella further. He glanced up, amusement and something akin to anger sparking in his eyes. Yes, he knew I considered him my rival—and he reveled in that. But his anger surprised me. Until Ella stepped back, and I saw her trembling hands.

"I'm not going to hurt her," I said, my tone waspish.

Philip raised his eyebrows. "That's where you're wrong, mate. You already have." He turned back to Ella leaned in a little closer. "Think about what I said."

She nodded. "Bye, Philip. And thank you again for the outing. Jeremiah and I enjoyed it. Very much."

He squeezed her gloved fingers one last time. "Anything to make you happy, El-Bel." The polite British bastard inclined his head toward me before heading back down the short walkway to his large silver SUV. A Land Rover, naturally.

"Didn't think Brits drove big vehicles," I said.

"He doesn't, normally. But he wanted to take all of us to the show up in the Cotswolds, and we didn't fit in a regular sedan, so he bought that one."

"Of course he did." Rich, arrogant wife stealer.

Wait. I could make purchases like that now, too. And it's not like Ella ever asked me to do something like that—I'd just hated

I couldn't give her the same lifestyle Asher provided for Lia and their kids.

"Where's the Audi?"

"In the garage."

Of course. I scrubbed my palms over my eyes, down my cheeks, hating these emotions ripping at me.

"Jeremiah won't even talk to me."

"He's angry." Ella said, stepping fully into the house and shutting the door with a quiet firmness.

"What did you tell him?" I asked, suspicious now. Jeremiah seemed to like Philip, which was out of character for him. Jeremiah and I had always been close.

CHAPTER SEVEN
Ella

"Not one damn thing." Did he really think I'd speak ill to Jeremiah about his own father?

Much as I wanted to shove Simon, I didn't. Mainly because I didn't trust myself to touch him. I'd missed his scent, his heat, the feel of his callused fingers on my lips, throat, breasts. Time to shut down that thought. Right now. Bringing forth the memory of Monique wrapped around Simon, her lips pressed to his, doused my need, leaving me cold and weary.

"Jeremiah's always loved me—"

"He still does."

I pulled off my gloves and struggled out of my coat. Simon took a step forward as though to help, but I shook my head hard. I couldn't stand him to touch me. Not now that he'd been with Monique. My skin crawled and my insides ached. Had Simon slept with her, then come to my bed? Had our baby been made after he started his affair? After knowing he planned to leave me? I settled onto the edge of a chair, my knees weak and unable to support me.

"—and he wouldn't avoid me unless you told him something. Does it have something to do with your new lover?"

"What?"

"Philip. I've seen the pictures, Ella. Didn't think you could hide how you ran right into your ex's arms, did you?"

If my mouth hadn't already fallen open, I might have been able to lock my jaw against the next words. "You—the man who *flaunted* his new lover in front of both your son and me—are going to claim that *I* did something wrong when I hugged an old friend?" I turned away. "Just get out."

"No. I'm not leaving this house until I talk to my son. Not until I have the proper documentation to prove the child you're carrying is—"

"Get out!" I screamed, standing up, my hands fisted at my sides. "Get out of my parents' house and don't ever contact me again. Ever."

Simon's flushed cheeks and narrowed eyes fell into a slack mask of shock. My temper was slow to burn, but once it ignited, it burned white hot and incinerated everyone in the vicinity.

"You lying, cheating scum!" I kicked him in the shin, hard. "I said get out. I don't want to hear one more word from you."

"Too damn bad. I want to know about the baby—"

"Then you should've asked before you decided to divorce me." My voice was high-pitched and sharp.

"You didn't tell me you were pregnant," he growled back.

"Because you were busy kissing and cuddling with your publicist—that's what *I* was dealing with along with weeks of bleeding, so I wasn't sure I'd *stay* pregnant."

Concern flickered in his eyes. "Is the baby okay?"

"You have no right to *ask* me anything about *my* children."

"I'm not giving up rights to my kids, Ella. They're mine."

"A moment ago, you inferred I was pregnant by another man. One I haven't seen, in person, in over ten years." The anger and the hurt, humiliation built in my chest, a pressure cooker about to explode. "Get out!" I pointed to the door with a trembling finger.

"When you get back to Seattle, we can discuss our—"

"We're staying here."

Simon's eyes narrowed again so that the hazel was barely visible behind his dark lashes.

"You'd do that?" His voice was soft. "Try to keep me from my kids? And...what? Install them with Philip as the loving father?"

I bit my lip hard enough to draw blood, my ears ringing with anger. "Considering you've spent exactly five days with Jeremiah in the last six months, I'm not doing *anything* to you."

Since Simon refused to leave, I swept from the room and headed up the stairs.

"This conversation isn't over," Simon said from much too near.

I hurried up the last steps and darted into my bedroom, slamming and locking the door just before his hand slapped against the wood.

Staying in England? Where had that come from?

"Open the door!" Simon roared.

No way I'd do that. From the sounds, I guessed Simon slid down to sit outside the door. A quick peek to the gap between door and carpet proved me right.

"What's happening?" Simon asked, his voice filled with bewilderment.

"You quit us," I whispered, my arms wrapped round my middle. "Chucked us out of your life like one would rubbish, and somehow expected everything else to stay the same."

Simon didn't give any indication he heard me nor did I hear movement implying he'd gotten up. I stood by the window for a while, watching people hurry through the cold, wet December rain. Eventually, standing became too much for the ligaments around my pelvis, and I flopped onto my bed. Doing my best to ignore his continued presence, I picked up my e-reader and opened Lia's newest novel.

"What are you still doing here?" Jeremiah asked. "Mom told you to leave."

I turned on my side, straining to hear Simon's answer.

"I wanted to see you," he said.

"I don't want to see you. And…and…I *hate* you."

My heart ached as I heard Jeremiah's feet stomp toward his room. His door rattled in its frame with the force of his slam. I heard a *thunk*, and I assumed Simon had dropped his head back against the wall.

I debated whether to go out to speak to him, but before I'd gathered enough courage to climb off the bed, I heard my father say, "You've done quite enough for today, young man."

"I need to talk to Ella," Simon said, his voice quiet with defeat.

"The time for that was *before* you embarrassed and hurt her by filing for divorce."

"I didn't…"

"It's time for you to go." My father's voice was firm. "And I'd strongly consider going back to that big life you now lead. Because you've destroyed what little bit of Christmas spirit Marsha and I've instilled in the kids."

I didn't hear anything else because I covered my head with my pillow, unable to listen to more.

When I finally stood, blackness encroached on the edges of my vision, lengthening the shadows on the walls and floor. I blinked it away as I staggered toward my door. Skipping breakfast was silly, and now I'd long-past missed lunch. Not healthy for either baby or me. I unlocked and opened the door, intending to check on Jeremiah. His angry words were so atypical—I couldn't begin to imagine the hurt and fear flooding through his system.

Opening the door, the faintness returned, stronger than before. This time, I didn't manage to grasp the door handle or the frame.

I slid forward with a soft groan. I jerked back, managing to bang my elbow on the doorframe before landing hard on my bottom.

"Mom! Are you okay? What did you hit?"

All the air was knocked from my lungs and my head swayed on my neck like I was three sheets to an unseen wind.

"Gramps! Gran!"

Feet pounded up the steps, and their anxious voices filled the room, all three of them speaking over and around me. I blinked up at them, still struggling to drag air into my lungs.

"I'm fine," I managed to wheeze out.

"No, you're not. We're off to hospital," Mum said. Her arm was around my shoulder, but I didn't remember her holding me. I placed my hand over my stomach, worry churning through my stomach.

"Okay."

"Right. Up you go." My father helped me to my feet, and I swayed with ponderous intent. Jeremiah was there, propping me up with this bony shoulder under my arm. My poor boy. He'd had so much change foisted upon his narrow, too-young shoulders. I'd have to do better, be better at protecting him.

Later. After I could manage stairs on my own.

———◆———

"Dehydration and low blood sugar." My mother clucked as

she pulled the thin hospital blankets up to my chin. "At least no bleeding this go-round. Simon's pop-in clearly didn't help."

No, it hadn't, especially once he basically accused me of cheating on him. The hypocritical arse.

"When's the nurse coming back to draw my blood?" I asked. I flicked at the blankets with fretful energy. I wanted to go home, but that wouldn't happen for many hours yet.

"Not till you're fully hydrated, love. Another hour or two."

Mum settled into the chair next to the bed, pulling out a large novel from her purse. She loved the historical fiction works— tomes I'd tried to get her to download onto the e-reader I'd bought her a couple of years ago for her transatlantic flights. She resisted, stating she preferred the physical manifestations.

"Where are Dad and Jeremiah?" I asked before she opened the book.

She glanced over her small reading spectacles, eyeing me with concern.

"Your father thought Jeremiah might prefer to go home now that we know you and the baby are all right. Seventeen weeks along. I can't believe you didn't know you were pregnant for the first trimester."

"We've tried for so long, Mum. And my periods haven't been regular since…" I trailed off, hating to think of the two miscarriages I'd struggled through in the past twelve years.

Mum wrapped her hand around mine, stroking the back of my hand with her thumb. "There, now. No reason to fret. The doctor said her heart rate is perfect."

I leaned back against the pillows. The baby was healthy. I was getting healthy. I had Jeremiah. I could do this. Somehow, I'd pick up the pieces of my life and be okay. Somehow.

Mum picked up her book and began to read. I must have dozed off because the next moment the nurse was checking my pulse. After noting it in the chart, she pulled out a syringe and began to draw blood.

"Is that for the paternity test?" I asked.

Mum made a disgruntled noise behind the book but didn't bother to look up.

The nurse nodded, watching the syringe. "Yes, NIPP we call it. Non-invasive prenatal paternity. We'll need the father's blood to compare it to."

"Will you call Simon, Mum? Ask him to offer up a sample so that he can be sure?"

"I am sure." His voice startled me as I turned to see him in the doorway to my room, looking even more tired and wan than he had this morning. If he'd just flown in today, his circadian rhythms must be mess. Not that I cared. Not my problem.

Monique could look after him—or not.

The nurse pulled out the needle and capped the syringe, taping my name to the label.

"You requested proof that this baby is yours, so get the test done. Maybe the nurse will be good enough to do it now," I said with a negligent wave I didn't much feel.

My mother shot me a glance, probably to tell me I wasn't behaving well, but I no longer cared. Beyond the hurt was a deep, roiling anger I wasn't sure I'd ever appease—this betrayal ripped too deep for healing.

"I believe you, Ella," Simon said on a heavy sigh.

I raised my eyebrows. "Not good enough for the attorneys,

I'm sure." I turned my head from him.

The nurse patted my arm before she headed to the door. "If you'll follow me, I'll show you where you go for the draw."

I ignored him, and finally his footsteps shuffled down the hall.

"That wasn't kind, Ella."

I pressed my lips together to stifle my trembling chin. "I don't care."

Mum reached over and squeezed my hand. "You sure about that? Because I can see how much you're hurting."

I turned away from her, too, curling onto my side.

———◆———

I woke again later, groggy and disoriented.

Right, I was in hospital. I pressed my hand to my growing bump.

"We'll be okay, my love. You, me, and Jeremiah. You'll see. This is just a bump in the road. A new reality to get used to. Once Jeremiah and I do, you'll see us happy again."

Simon's despondent voice filled the room. "Do you hate me that much, Ella?"

CHAPTER EIGHT
Simon

I lifted my head from where it rested against my chest. Her head whipped toward me, her eyes sheening over as she clamped her jaw tight. We stared at each other for a long moment. Her eyes hardened with each beep of the monitor, but she continued to rest her palms on her belly. Protecting the life within. *From me.*

I knotted my hands into fists, trying to stave off the rush of emotion clogging my throat and lashing at my heart. The rhythm stuttered as Ella's eyes slid closed, shutting me out.

The guilt of not being there for her, not being able to hold her at night or kiss those rosy lips each morning—missing yet another goal Jeremiah scored, and seeing his bright grin—the reasons I'd given myself and the lawyer for the divorce faded under the weight of this newer, deeper pain.

"Why are you here?" Ella asked.

My heart trilled at Ella's voice, even if her tone remained clipped. "Your mother called me. I'm your next of kin." That sounded harsh. Why did everything seem to come out wrong? "I needed to make sure you were okay. That the baby…our daughter is going to be fine."

She flicked the cord of her IV. "So *now* she's your daughter. Could be I was having a raving affair with one of the teachers at school, or maybe one of Asher's friends. Or…I know! Seeing as how you accused me of something salacious, I'm having one of my students' babies."

"Ella." My voice cracked on her name. "I'm sorry."

She glared but the hurt still blossomed from her tired, puffy eyes. "You bloody well should be."

"I was jealous." I rasped out the words. My throat dry, my voice scratchy.

"Of what? Why?" she cried. "You're…you're the one having an affair!" With a thick swallow and a wet sniffle, she turned her head away. "You're the one who tossed me over."

Ella would think that—and why not? Damn Monique these past few months. Her manipulations wreaked havoc on our lives. "I'm not. I never cheated on you."

Her head whipped back around, and my chest ached as tears dripped over her lower lashes. "Bullshit, Simon. I'm many things but stupid is not one of them." She swiped hard at her wet cheeks. "I saw those pictures months ago. When I asked you, you said not to worry. Not an issue. But, here we are—you asking for divorce and kissing that…that…woman in front of me." Her chin trembled and her hands fisted. "How could you?"

I scooted forward on my chair, needing her to see the sincerity in my eyes. "I never had sex with another woman, Ella. From the day I met you on that cricket pitch at Cambridge, I've been faithful to you."

"And, yet, you planned to leave me. Because I no longer fit your life." She pushed herself up on her elbows. One of the monitors began to beep with a more rapid, insistent beat. "You've already chucked us to streamline your touring. Well, believe me, I don't want to be part of that world—or part of yours since you've proved we're so easy to drop."

"It wasn't like that. And now with the baby…"

"She's not your concern. Neither is Jeremiah nor me."

I sat back in the chair, air leaking from my lungs as if I'd been slugged in the chest.

"You'd keep her from me?"

Ella narrowed her eyes, the beeping ratcheting up again. "Just…go back to your famous life and rub elbows with all those bloody famous arses, but do not expect me to believe *anything* that comes out of your ruddy, duplicitous mouth again."

Two nurses rushed into the room, followed by a doctor.

The older nurse shooed me from the chair. "We need you to step outside."

I rose, my heart pounding as fast as Ella's was. "Is she okay? What about the baby?"

"Out, sir."

The doctor picked up a device and placed it on Ella's naked belly. The slight curve there slowed my steps, and I gawped. Ella's loose sweater hid both the tiny tummy bulge and the sharp peaks of her hip bones. When the doctor raised her gown higher, her skin showed each indentation of ribs.

She hadn't looked like that last time we were together—before those pictures of Monique came out, before she began to pull away, and I let her. I let her because it was easier than dealing with her jealousy and fears. Easier just to brush them off. But… seeing her so thin and heartbroken. My own heart cracked wide.

"Oh, Ella," I whispered, but she didn't hear my concern, too busy crying harder as the doctor listened to the baby's heartbeat.

"Nice and steady," he said, patting her thin shoulder.

"Out!" The nurse prodded me hard with her index finger. Once through the door, I turned back in time to have the wooden edge clip the tip of my nose.

CHAPTER NINE
Ella

Opening my eyes, I blinked against the deep pulsing in my head. My hand immediately cradled my stomach, reassuring myself of the baby within. I glanced over at the fetal-heart-rate monitor the doctor prescribed after the scare that sent Simon from my room. A small yip fell from my lips.

"Sorry. Didn't mean to scare you," the young woman said. She stood and faced me. "The baby's heart rate's been nice and consistent."

"You're American," I said. An admittedly stupid comment. "And you're not dressed like my nurse."

"Right on both accounts."

The young woman's conservative spectacles glinted green from the monitors next to my bed, her long, blond hair falling out of what was once a chignon at the base of her neck.

"I knew you had to be smart," she said with a smile.

"And you are?"

"Angelica Gatlin. I work for the record studio."

My breathing escalated, and I clutched at the sheets covering my chest. Simon must have sent this young woman—to what? Butter me up? No way.

"Please leave. I don't want you in here."

She stepped forward into better light. Her skin slid over her cheekbones and to her neck in the smooth elegance of youth, but her eyes held secrets behind the chunky black frames.

"I'm here to help."

"Seeing as how the record label is part of the reason my life is a complete disaster, I'm not sure there's one thing you could do to help at this point," I said, voice tart.

"Asher Smith called my boss. He's not happy with Simon's ex-publicist. Neither is my boss. That's why I'm here." She smiled again. "I'm here to set right something that never should have happened."

"Oh?" I replied, eyebrows raised. "What's that?"

Her lips quirked as she shook her head. "I'd rather not say just yet."

"Then it's best for you to leave." My mind spun with how to control the article sure to come from Angelica's snooping in my hospital room. My stomach roiled in matching pitch to my throbbing head.

Angelica studied me for a minute. "You look done in."

"You've no idea."

Angelica smiled—a bright flash of teeth that left my chest hollow. At least someone had something to smile about. "Just so you know, Simon called right after that scene at the festival in Atlanta. He's a mess."

I crossed my arms over my belly, needing the reassurance of my bump. "Did you kiss him, too?"

Angelica skittered back a little, eyes opening wider with shock. "Um, no. I don't—"

"You're about the same age as that other woman—Monique. Perhaps you've decided to share him?" My voice remained level but my tone bit just as I wanted it to. The younger woman flinched.

I don't trust you.

"Mrs. Dorsey, I'd never do that."

"Then you're about the only woman who wouldn't."

She stepped in closer, her feet shuffling. "I-I just meant Simon seemed upset after your departure. Like, really torn up."

"No longer my concern, Angelica. He'll figure out his way forward." Without me. Without us. "He always does."

"He clearly never figured you out," Angelica said. "You'd absolutely do it. Even though you still love him. You'd never see him again."

I pressed my lips together to keep my chin from trembling.

"What about your son? And, now, daughter? Do they deserve to live a life without him in it?"

With that parting shot, she strolled out my door.

The ambitious young lady made a valid point.

CHAPTER TEN
Simon

I stopped at the edge of the waiting area, annoyed but unsurprised to see Philip sitting with Marsha and Dave. Jeremiah leaned his head back against the wall, phone in hand, probably playing one of those shooting games he'd come to love. I forced my feet forward and stiffened my spine when Dave's cold eye landed on me.

For a quick moment, Jeremiah's eyes brightened with joy before his mouth firmed and he dropped his gaze back to his device. My confidence faltered as the pain of my son's ready dismissal snaked through me.

"Is Ella still sleeping?" I asked.

Marsha nodded, her face pale and her eyes dimmed with worry. She fidgeted, her hands wrapping around each other in indecision before Dave settled his hand over hers, stilling the reaction.

My father-in-law glowered. "The doctor says Ella can't abide additional stresses. You, Simon, are the source of her stress. The reason she collapsed at the house and the reason the doctor's now so concerned about her blood pressure. If you care about my daughter—and *your* daughter—at all, the best thing you can do is leave Ella alone."

I sucked in my lips as I absorbed that blow. The concern for my unborn baby ate at me, but just as worrisome was Ella's health. Jeremiah needed her…and so did I.

"I want to know how she's doing," I managed to say. "Ella and *our daughter* are my primary concern."

"Then you should have thought about her feelings before!"

I swiveled to face my son, whose eyes narrowed in dangerous Ella fashion, but the belligerent stance and set lips were all me.

"I do care about Ella's feelings," I said, keeping my voice low, soothing. But panic and anger bubbled up. Why did Philip's lips quirk up in a faint smile? I'd disliked his relationship with Ella before, not that they had much of one—an occasional email, the passing mention of his name when she was on her social media, catching up with her friends from uni. But now...him here, comforting Ella's parents, Jeremiah's willingness to have him close, pissed me off.

"If you'd loved Mom, you wouldn't want a divorce. And if you loved Mom, you wouldn't be screwing that ugly cow you were with the other day."

"Whoa." I raised my hands. "First off, I'm not screwing anyone, and second that's no way to talk about Monique."

Jeremiah stood, and I realized we were almost eye-to-eye. When had he grown so tall? How much of his childhood had I missed? How much would I continue to miss because of my career?

"Would you prefer I called her a slut? How about clingy, cheating bi—"

"While I couldn't agree more with the sentiment," a young blond woman said, bustling into the room, "probably best not to say it here, when reporters are lurking just down the hall. Their ears—via microphone, you know, like those of the Weasley brothers in *The Order of the Phoenix*?—yeah, these ears put those to shame."

Jeremiah blinked at the woman, probably shocked by the Harry Potter reference as much as the attempt to use humor as a warning. Jeremiah settled back, his mouth twisted in a surly line.

"Angelica?" I asked.

She offered me a fine-boned hand. "Yes. Angelica Gatlin. Your newest team member, and Jon Singer's personal fixer-upper."

Part of me wanted to blame Jon for getting me in this mess in the first place—he helped put together my team, set up my tour schedule. And I'd been off-balance—trying to find my equilibrium—since I started this tour schedule. Shouldn't that have told me something? I obviously needed more time with my wife to ground me.

I glanced over at Philip, who'd continued to relax in his chair, one leg propped on the other knee. An urbane businessman, well pleased with his position in the world.

"We need to talk," she said, causing Jeremiah to snort and sink farther into his seat, and Dave to raise his brows high, his jowls quivering in indignation.

"Good one, Dad. Just bring your latest sl—"

"What did you want to talk with me about?" I said on a sigh, unwilling to hear the rest of Jeremiah's words. Marsha and Dave wouldn't reprimand him for the use, and clearly I had no sway with discipline.

Angelica glanced at the other people in the room, her eyes narrowed in suspicion as they landed on Philip. At least she and I agreed on him.

"You want me to tell you in here—in front of all these people?"

"Considering my son and father-in-law think I'm having a torrid affair with you, yes, I think that would be best."

"Ick." Angelica's jaw snapped shut and her cheeks turned redder than the Santa decorations I'd passed on my way in.

"That's not…We're not…Oh, my goodness. I've never even met you until just now." She brought her hand up to her cheek and pressed it there, hard. "So, um, I wanted to let you know that Monique is suing you."

I rocked back on my heels. "For what, exactly?"

"Attention."

I almost smiled at that, but then the reality of the situation hit me: my brand, my image as a musician was about to take another hit.

"She didn't say anything about us having a relationship, did she?" I growled. "We do *not* have a relationship."

Angelica tilted her head. "False termination. She said she's the one who's managed your career and you misled her into believing she was going to be your manager…and your wife." Angelica shrugged, her face apologetic.

"Well, she's never going to be either. That's why I fired her." Christ. My hands balled into fists and I inhaled slowly only to exhale more slowly. My heart rate remained too rapid.

The situation here, with Ella and the baby, was tenuous. I pressed my thumbs to my eye sockets.

"I appreciate the heads-up."

Angelica dropped her hand to my shoulder. "You're not the first person Monique's hurt. You probably won't be the last."

I dropped my hands and shook out my arms, causing Angelica's hand to fall from my body. I didn't want her touch. I wanted Ella's, and I wasn't sure she'd ever touch me for comfort again. "Thanks, again. I'll talk to Jon about all this."

Angelica nodded, but she looked abashed. "Um. About that."

"What did you do?"

"Well…Jon and I are now aware you hadn't been looped in on the decision-making these past few months." She shrugged, her eyes darting toward Jeremiah, who'd lifted his head to listen with more interest.

"We're sifting through all of Monique and Gerard's messages for the last year. We have messages between the two of them changing your schedule, adding tour dates to your calendar without first getting your sign off. We also have a correspondence between them suggesting that the added tours, the time away from your family, might get Ella out of the picture. Nothing definitive yet on their involvement in the divorce."

Marsha let out a small, startled gasp, and Dave grunted, shoving his feet forward hard against the tile. Philip laid his arm across the back of the next chair.

"Probably best you fired the woman," Philip said. "And doesn't sound like she has much of a case."

Angelica turned a megawatt grin at Philip who blinked a couple of times.

No, Angelica, we don't like him.

"Exactly. That's what my staff and I are working on now."

I didn't know whether to strangle the young woman or hug her. I settled for a brief nod.

"Shouldn't take long to sort out. Monique wants the attention—notoriety—she knows she isn't going to win the case, but she wouldn't be opposed to a fat settlement." Angelica drew herself up and scowled. "Which I've been assured by both Jon and legal that she will *not* be getting." She cleared her throat, her eyes darting around the room before she smiled and turned on her heel.

Silence hung thick in the air. A nurse came around the corner and smiled at Dave and Marsha. "Ella's awake and the doctor's finished examining her. She asked to see her son and both of you." She tipped her head toward Ella's parents.

Marsha rose with Dave's help, looking older, more fragile. Probably something else I needed to shoulder the blame for. At the last minute, Marsha turned back and glanced at me. "You want to come in? See her?"

"I don't want to upset her more. Will you let me know how she looks? If she's eating? I'm worried. She's lost weight since Halloween…" The last time I spent time with my wife. Halloween. I rolled my head back on my neck.

Philip shoved his feet out in front of him, reminding me he was still in the room, devouring the strange tableau of my family disintegrating.

"Jeremiah?" Dave asked.

"I'll come in a minute," he said.

I turned to find his gaze locked on my face as I settled into a chair two down from his. I linked my hands between my knees and waited, trying to brace my heart for the next barrage of anger.

Jeremiah bit his lip and stood, eyes still on me. He crossed over and dropped into the chair next to mine.

"So, you didn't? Have…um, well, you didn't cheat on Mom?"

I met his eyes, held the look for a long moment before I shook my head once. "No, son. I'd never do that to your mother."

"She thinks you did. And she's cried when she goes to bed. She's upset you haven't called regularly. That's been going on for weeks, Dad. And…and I heard what Monique said, calling you baby. I saw you kiss her."

I sighed and closed my eyes briefly, but I opened them again to focus on my son's face, his own eyes beseeching me not to have let him down.

"I love your mother, Miah," I said, drawing on the nickname we rarely used. "She—and you, now the baby—are the best things to ever happen to me. Ever." I kept my gaze firm.

"But you want to divorce her. Break up our family."

I shook my head, maintaining the eye contact. "No. I considered it briefly after your mother quit taking my calls when that first photo came out, showing me with Monique."

Clearly, my dismissing Ella's concerns out-of-hand had been stupid. But, how could she think I'd ever look at another woman? Ella was…well, she was my life. Had been for nearly two decades. Still, I should have been smarter, reassured her more, when she came to me with her initial concern. Instead, I became defensive and angry—which led me into my lawyer's office and put me on the path to sitting here, in this waiting room, having a painful conversation with my son.

"Mom wants to stay here. She's too sad to go back. And embarrassed." Jeremiah's eyes narrowed, his face hardening. "Sending the papers to her school was *mean*."

I cleared my throat. "I didn't ask for the papers to be drawn up, let alone sent. Monique did. That's why I fired her. That and because she kissed me, which hurt you and your mother."

Jeremiah's mouth twisted. "One of the benefits of so many friends whose parents are divorced is we know stuff. Like the fact you had to contact the lawyer to start a divorce proceeding. You had to set up a meeting to discuss the terms."

I squeezed my hands together tighter. My fingertips tingled.

"You're right. I did. I thought that was the right thing for you. For Ella."

Jeremiah shoved out of his seat in disgust. He turned back to face me, the anger and despair mingling in his eyes and his voice. "Then how can you say you love my mom? Or me? You *planned* to leave us permanently. You called to set that up." He didn't bother to look back as he trotted down the hall toward Ella's room.

After another long moment of trying to breathe through the ache in my chest, I turned my head to look at Philip.

"I was always jealous you had her first. And I'm pissed off you saw all that. That you can exploit it when you go after her again."

Philip considered me for a long moment, causing my palms to sweat. "She married you."

I placed my hands on my knees. "You still love her?"

Philip's mouth flipped up in a sardonic twist. "Enough to put up with you."

He shoved his hands in his slacks and walked down the hall after my son, leaving me alone in the waiting room.

———◆———

Angelica slid into the chair next to me. A notepad in her lap and a pen poised over the yellow, lined paper.

"It's all over the music news. They're pestering the label, Asher Smith and his family, your wife's coworkers…anyone they can think of for a statement. So, give me a statement. Now. That's *why* I'm in England. To fix this mess."

I turned my head and shot her the look my former students knew to fear. "Ella's very sick. We're worried about the baby—and

El. The rest…Monique, the tour…I can't focus on that now. We've tried for this child for *years*. I've gotta be here for Ella right now."

Angelica wiggled in her chair. "Of course you do. Thank the music gods you're a decent man because I've had to deal with one too many pieces of shit who only care about how much is in the bank and how many women they can dick over."

"Well…" I cleared my throat. My heart thumped hard then skipped a beat. I glanced up at the sound of footfalls in time to see Marsha pause in the entrance to the room. I dropped my eyes back to my feet, unable to bear her shaming looks. "I did screw up. Bad. Gerard and Monique suggested I contact my lawyer about a divorce. I did that. I went so far as to lay out some terms. *Preliminary* terms. But I never followed up."

"So, are you planning to leave Ella, Simon?" Marsha's voice filled with disapproval. My shoulders bunched back into the thick knots of the past few days.

"I have to tell you, based on your music, this is not going to go over well with your fans," Angelica said.

"I don't care about the fans," I snapped. "I mean, I do. Of course. But the people I'm most concerned about are my wife and children. Monique hurt them." I sucked in a breath, released it on a heavy sigh. Angelica knew this but Marsha didn't understand the whole story. "I contacted my lawyer as soon as Ella left Atlanta. He sent me an email from my account, signed *by me* stating that I wanted those papers delivered to Ella last week. Only problem is *I* don't have that email in my files—anywhere—and I didn't send it."

"You're sure? You didn't get high or drunk and do it?" Marsha asked.

"I'm positive." I raised my gaze and met Marsha's. "I never sent that message to my lawyer. I absolutely was the one to contact him initially, but I never planned to follow through. I told him that at the end of the meeting."

Angelica's soft huff blasted across my skin, and I jerked, shocked. I'd forgotten she was there, next to me, but the moment between Marsha and I also snapped without me getting a good read on her expression—and whether she believed me.

"Look," Angelica nearly groaned the word. "Whatever you did with Monique is in the past. The label has severed our professional relationship with her. It's not just you—we've had a few reports over the past few months. Just that you were her main client. Jon definitely sat up when Asher called, though."

My brother-in-law came through. Big time. I owed him.

"That's good. Monique clearly has ethical deficiencies.

Angelica barked out a laugh. "Ethical deficiencies were created by musicians. And actors."

I turned to face Angelica, meeting her brown eyes behind those no-nonsense black frames. "I'm not coming back to my tour until I'm sure Ella and our daughter are healthy. I don't know when that'll be. If you need to severe our relationship, sue me for breach, do it. But I'm not leaving my wife."

Angelica rolled her eyes and slammed her pen against the notepad. "Get a grip, Simon. We don't have any plans to cut you from the label. *Yet*. I've spoken with Jon and I've already gotten you out of the rest of your concerts for December and the first two weeks of January."

"I'm not sure—"

Angelica raised her hand. I stopped speaking. "By then, you

need to get back on the tour with a new, better team in place. Jon wants photo ops with your family—everyone will eat up the baby bump—and I think that's a good idea. The first step to fixing a mess that, whether you agree or not, *you* created." She tapped her pen on the empty page. "Can you do that?"

"I don't know. I'll try."

"Good enough for now." Angelica tucked her notepad under her arm. "Don't screw this up." She nodded to Marsha before bustling down the hallway, phone already to her ear.

I cradled my head between my hands.

Marsha settled into a chair next to me, her light perfume teasing my nose. Ella didn't wear perfume. She said it gave her hives. But I'd decided years before she wanted to stake a claim that was different from the persona of her mother. Hence, the lack of perfume and embracement of ripped jeans, cowboy boots, and multiple earrings in just her right ear. Small rebellions that Marsha hated, but proved a necessary point.

Ones Jeremiah would throw at Ella and me soon enough. Maybe Ella was already dealing with them—I didn't know.

I gritted my teeth. So many regrets.

Fame, for me, hadn't proved the panacea I'd dreamed.

"I can't say I approve of these past few weeks," Marsha began on a choked breath. "Ella called me, you know. When that first photo came out. She was beside herself with worry."

I waited. No reason to rush her, especially seeing as how she wasn't angry or accusatory. Yet.

"You hurt my daughter, Simon. I might even say you broke her." Marsha paused. I glanced over to see her settle her purse in her lap. "I preferred Philip, you know. Over you. Both Dave and I did. Not because I couldn't see how much Ella loved you—everyone's always seen that fierceness. The only one she might love more is Jeremiah, but I think even he knows you're her true love."

I slumped farther into the chair's unforgiving plastic cushion. "I know you're disappointed in me."

Marsha patted my shoulder. "Every generation acts as if they're the first to discover sex and to discover arguments." She chortled, but the brief sound cut off on a sigh. "Neither is accurate. But I wanted you to know I see now why Ella chose you—and I still wish she'd have chosen Philip. He can't break her heart as you've done."

I squeezed my hands together, angry my mother-in-law needed to tell me I was well behind as her top choice.

"Philip can be a shoulder for her to cry on right now, but he'll never be Ella's mate, her partner. That's *always* been you."

My guts pulled in multiple directions. Marsha believed I was Ella's true love. "I never wanted to hurt her. Or Jeremiah."

"Hmm. You were in my home yelling awful accusations yesterday. Seems you did plan on hurting someone."

Marsha gathered up her purse and stood, moving toward the sound of voices bouncing off the sterile tiled walls. Dave and Jeremiah, by the sounds of it. Where was Philip?

Marsha turned her face back over her shoulder. "You claim to love Ella, still. You need to prove it, Simon. Not just to me or Dave or even Jeremiah." Her lips pressed flat. "And definitely not to the world at large. They don't matter, not really."

She walked to Dave and Jeremiah, wrapping her arm around my son, who didn't bother to look back.

———— • ————

I tiptoed down the hallway, concerned about what I'd overhear—or worse, see—between Ella and Philip.

I breathed out a deep sigh of relief. Ella lay in her bed, eyes closed. Alone.

"The doctors said it's touch-and-go, you know."

I glanced at Angelica. "You scared me. I thought you'd left."

She snorted. "Please. I'm on the clock until this is sorted to Jon's satisfaction." She raised her eyebrows.

"How do you know that? About Ella?"

Angelica shrugged, eyes on Ella's sleeping form. "I hear things. I see things." Her lips curved up in a hint of a smile. "I know things."

I slid my hands into my pockets and rocked back on my heels. "You seem to know an awful lot about me."

Her smile grew. "You're my current project."

"Do you care?" I turned to face her fully. My frustration spilling out into the words I threw at her. "About Ella? My son? Or is this all to make sure I look good, so the record label looks good?"

She turned toward me and her eyes darkened, the smile leaving her lips. "Oh, I care. Not so much for you, really."

I absorbed that blow.

The one person who'd been nice, helpful, and I'd not even said thank you to her.

Angelica waved her hand in front of her face. "Do you have any idea how hard it is to be left behind? My father, Major Gatlin, did that."

"Major Gatlin? The guy who used to tour with—"

"Yes. Major was my father. I didn't see him for the last five years of his life—not once."

I rocked back on my heels, my guts seeming to fall onto the floor. "Angelica, I'm so sorry."

She studied me. For the first time, her face was wan, tired. Her eyes no longer bright. She dipped her head. "I survived."

I turned back to look through the small window in the door. Ella's waist dipped in before flaring out over her hip. Her chest rose and fell in a steady rhythm. From here, she didn't look pregnant. And she didn't look old enough to be my wife of fifteen years. She'd always been so capable—ready to make others laugh, to take on another assignment, committee, a ten-boy sleepover in the park. Whatever needed doing, Ella managed.

Her chest stuttered and my heart ached.

"Ella's been my muse and my rock for so long. How did I lose sight of that?"

Angelica turned back toward me, her brows pinched tight over her nose and her lips pursed in annoyance. "I think the better question is, why do you get to live your dream at the expense of your family?"

CHAPTER ELEVEN
Ella

I hadn't seen Simon yet today, and his absence left me tetchy. I had a huge bouquet from him—and another from Lia, Asher, Briar, and Hayden. Both were lovely and smelled delightful. Based on the weight of Simon's bouquet, he might have bought out the entire floral shop, but the arrangement was tasteful and held all my favorites.

At least he remembered my love for ranunculus. And peonies. And...sigh, yes, those feathery tulips I adored. I'd made him go to the tulip festival in a small town north of Seattle with me not once, but twice. Jeremiah ran through the rows pretending to be a crop duster while I stopped to touch each flower, to take a million pictures.

Each time, Simon smiled and bought me a big bouquet to commemorate the trip.

We hadn't gone in the last five—maybe six—years.

I rolled my eyes as I edged to side of the bed and set my booted feet on the floor. The tulips were a nice touch, but he should have remembered I promised to love him till death did part us.

Now, though, after being blindsided by his desire to be well-rid of me, could I ever trust him again?

Therein lay the crux of the whole matter.

"Ready, then, love?"

Mum's bright voice belied the worry lines around her eyes and mouth. Not much I could do about those. Just as there wasn't much I could do to reduce my blood pressure or ensure the baby's continued development. Eating more would help. As would rest and relaxation, the doctor had said.

I'd do everything possible to ensure this gel's continued growth—to give her the best possible chance.

But rest? Relaxation? Not bloody likely now that I was in the middle of Simon's stupid media shit storm.

"Sure."

The nurse wheeled me out to the curb where Mum's car chortled. I slid into the beige leather front seat, refusing to look up into the myriad flashes or answer a single yelled question.

"Bloody noisy bunch," Mum grumbled, jerking the wheel so we sped away from the hospital.

"It's news. Salacious news. And since Simon isn't with me, it's bigger news."

"Do you want him to be? With you, I mean."

I turned to look at her as she slowed for a stoplight. Mum turned her head toward me, the sunlight catching in her light-brown eyes, turning them molten.

"I don't know. A month ago? Absolutely."

"He's hurting, too."

I crossed my arms over my chest. "And that's supposed to make me feel better? He deserves to hurt."

Mum made a strangled sound in her throat. She tightened her grip on the wheel and pressed us through the light.

My eyes filled with tears that I blinked back. "I don't know if I can forgive him."

"You always were deeply wrapped up in that boy. From the first moment I saw the two of you together, I worried."

"Really?" I tipped my head, taking in her puckered mouth.

"You want your children to find love and happiness, Ella. You know this. But getting lost in another person? That's dangerous."

Didn't I know it.

———————

I traced a snowflake down the edge of the car window's glass.

"Remember when Miah was born?" Mum asked.

"Of course. One of the worst snow days in Seattle history."

"I thought Simon was going to rip his heart out when your water broke. But he held it together and drove you to the hospital with such calm, even when you started shrieking about the pain from the contractions."

"Mmm. Glad we got there when we did. Those contractions were bloody awful."

In fact, they'd been worse than awful. But Simon stayed calm, holding my hand, offering me ice chips, and even rubbing my back when the pain intensified to the point I couldn't breathe through the labor pains.

"You've got this, El," he'd said over and over. He kissed my knuckles or brushed my hair back from my face, cupping my cheek. "I love you."

The memory crashed over me.

I missed those moments. I missed the man I'd always thought my husband was.

I bit my lower lip. He didn't come back to the hospital—no matter what he said about believing me that this child was his— he hadn't come back after he asked me if I hated him.

Part of me did, and I'm sure he knew it.

He knew because, until recently, we shared an intimacy I'd only seen in a rare few other couples. My sister-in-law Lia used to eye my relationship with Simon with such hunger, I felt guilty.

Then, she reconnected with Asher and she lived in her own wedded wonderland.

As my world—all its imperfect beauty with the constancy of song and laughter—began to collapse.

"He was scared, Ella. Frightened for both of you."

I made a noncommittal sound.

I wanted to go back to then.

The baby kicked.

No, I didn't. Then, I wouldn't have this child growing inside me.

Yet, even with the child inside me and my mother here, I'd never felt more alone.

CHAPTER TWELVE
Simon

I pulled into Dave and Marsha's drive as apprehension licked at my guts. I blew into my cupped hands, hoping the air would warm my stiff fingers. My stomach churned. My reception this morning was sure to be chillier than the air.

I walked to the front door and rang the bell. I rocked back on my heels and stared at the small, neat porch—a place I'd never stood before this visit. Ella and her family always entered the cottage via the kitchen door to the back of the house—a door I knew to almost always be unlocked and easy to open into the luscious smells of Marsha's baking.

Dave opened the door, book in hand, reading glasses perched low on his nose. A deep frown settling over his face. "Bloody hell. What do you want?"

"To take my son sledding." I pushed past Dave when he made to shut the door, my heart shoved up in my throat and my pulse beating mad thunks in my ears.

I jogged into the front room where Jeremiah lay on the hard settee, his phone inches from his nose. He sat up and scowled when he noticed me.

"We're going sledding," I said without preamble.

"Now, look here," Dave said from behind me. His bluster bit into my ears and confidence.

I kept my gaze firm on my son. "We haven't been in ages. Please, Miah."

Jeremiah's gaze darted from mine to Dave's and back a few times before he stood and nodded. "Mom needs to rest."

"I won't bother her now. I promise." I laid my hand over my heart.

Again, Jeremiah nodded, but his face pinched with concern. He bundled up into his winter gear while I promised Dave I'd have Jeremiah back in time for dinner.

We exited the house, and I grabbed the two wooden sleds from the trunk of the rental sedan. I pulled them by the ropes up the hill toward the park where most of the families in the area joined together for cocoa at the sledding hill. It was a bit early for the whole crew, but the hill would get more crowded as the week wore on.

The icy layer over the snow crunched before my foot slid deeper into the cold fluff. We walked, Jeremiah shooting me glances from the corner of his eye.

"I want your mother back," I said. "I want us to be the family we were. Before...before all the fame. The touring."

Jeremiah turned his face toward me, staring so hard, he stumbled over a broken piece of sidewalk. I caught his elbow, but he pulled free from my grip and tugged down his coat.

"I need your help," I said.

Jeremiah hurried ahead. We climbed the hill and stood there as the wind whipped at our hats, biting into my cheeks and lips. He turned to face me. His cheekbones stood out stark against the cool gray light, and his lashes—the ends tipped in that bit of gold—masked his eyes.

"I don't think that's a good idea," he said, his voice cracking.

I'd left last year when my son was still a boy. He stood before me now, looking much closer to a man.

Seven months of grueling moves night after night, and for

what? What had I gained? A fatter bank account? I looked at my son and grief clawed at my throat.

"I messed up. I messed up bad." My breath came out in random pants. "You hate me. Your mother resents me." I dropped my gaze and let me chin fall to my chest. "I thought fame and money would fix everything. I was wrong."

I forced my eyes back up to meet my son's. He studied me for a long moment, then another. Neither of us moved.

"We used to sit on the back porch and sing stupid songs about the clouds," Jeremiah said, his voice wistful. "You and Mom held hands and laughed."

We hadn't done that in over a year. Ella came up with the game years ago to help Jeremiah learn the types of clouds. He'd loved the songs she made up so much, I'd started singing about the clouds' shapes.

Some nights, we'd sit outside until well after dark, singing and laughing.

"I miss that, too." I scrubbed my hands over my bristly cheeks. "I got my priorities crossed. I've always had the most important pieces—you and your mom, now the baby, too. I want that. I want to be *with* you. For the soccer games, and recitals and first steps and crying in the night and…whatever. That's more important than a record deal or fans or…or anything else." The lump in my throat grew, making talking nearly impossible. "And I'm sorry I didn't see that when I should have. How I should have. I need you to know. I get it now, Miah. I get what I threw away."

His eyes hardened but his lips trembled. "You made us both feel really horrible, Dad."

Slowly, I pulled my son in, and as he fell against my shoulder,

I hugged him tighter, absorbing his sobs and his tears. I rested my cheek on his hat and let some of my own tears fall.

CHAPTER THIRTEEN
Ella

My legs ached from standing at the window, trying to be inconspicuous as I waited for Simon to return Jeremiah. He wouldn't take him—take my son from me—would he?

I inhaled in a sharp, annoyed breath. My thoughts jumped around, as unsteady as my hormones and my body.

With a sigh, I returned to the settee and flung the blanket over my cold feet, pulling it up over my chest. I picked up the bowl of steaming mushroom soup my mother brought me a few minutes earlier and dipped in my spoon, enjoying the aroma of thyme near as much as the rich, earthy taste. My mum was a smashing cook.

I set the now-empty bowl on the edge of the coffee table and closed my eyes. Beneath the excitement and love for my developing daughter resided a deep weariness. More than a decade past from my last successful pregnancy—my body had aged and needed more rest. But, perhaps equally as important, my mind needed to hide from the difficult choices I'd soon have to make.

I turned back to face the window, my eyes bleary from the exhaustion I couldn't outstrip.

Jeremiah's voice woke me. I jolted upright, nearly oversetting myself. I yelped, and flopped back onto the settee, my heart pounding.

Jeremiah stuck his head in the doorway.

"She's awake," he yelled back down the hall before stepping into the room and settling into the still-warm spot next to me. His cheeks held a note of pink from either exertion, cold, or fun.

"How are you feeling?"

"Fine." I dropped my hand from my heart and patted my hair. "So. Did you have a good time sledding?"

Jeremiah shrugged. "It was okay. Not much snow so we couldn't get up the speed. And no one else was there, which made it kinda boring."

I leaned over and brought him closer to my side. Jeremiah closed his eyes and leaned against me.

"Mom?"

"Yes?"

"I don't want to stay in England. I'm sure it's fun and all—I mean, the soccer's awesome and they play rugby and cricket— but if we stay here, I'll miss my friends. And I'll miss kayaking and rock climbing and hanging out with Aunt Lia and Uncle Asher and playing all the coolest new games with Mason and seeing Clay's band and…" he ran out of breath and shuddered.

He lifted his head up off my shoulder and pierced me with a pleading look. Within his eyes, his fear blossomed. Jeremiah dropped his gaze to his hands that he twisted into a knot over his knees. He blew out a breath and fidgeted. "I heard Gran telling Pop. That awful Monique lady sent an email from Dad's account to the lawyer."

"What?"

Jeremiah nodded. "Gran told Pop last night. That's why the suit already got dropped." Jeremiah pointed to the newspaper I hadn't bothered to pick up. I did now and read the article. Short and to the point: Monique Lanson's contract with Simon's record company was terminated, effective immediately for ethics violations and lies to the press.

I sat back against the settee, staring at the paper.

"Mom?"

"Yes?" I forced my gaze back up to my son's face.

"I think Dad still loves you. And the baby."

"I don't know what to say, Jeremiah."

"Will you think about going home after New Year's?"

"What if we do this?" I rubbed my palms across my thighs. "What if we let Dad spend time with you for as long as he's here. We'll see how it goes between him and me. And I promise not to uproot you from your friends and your life without discussing my reasons for doing so first."

Jeremiah hugged me, hard. His cheek pressed into my neck. "Thanks, Mom. Really. Thanks!"

He hopped off the settee and flew from the room. A whoop trailed behind him.

"I'm proud of you, Ella."

I started. Mum set down a plate of biscuits and a strong cup of tea. After a small hesitation, my mother settled into the space Jeremiah left. This time, she settled her arms around my shoulders.

"I had an affair, you know."

I turned to look at her, eyes wide and mouth gaping.

Her normally ruddy cheeks paled and her lips pressed tight. "You were five. I'd had a miscarriage and the doctor told us I couldn't have more children. Dave turned inward, toward you and making your world perfect, whereas I sought comfort—no, an escape from the pain of that loss—elsewhere."

Mum dabbed at her eyes with the handkerchief she kept in the pocket of her long woolen cardigan. My mother, an affair?

The world seemed mad. Sheer craziness had taken over. No way my mum cheated. But she'd told me she had. I pressed the heels of my hands to my temples and breathed.

"That's part of what your father is having such a hard time with now. Between you and Simon. He remembers how hard it was to trust me again, and he doesn't want that for you."

She laughed, but it was watery and a bit sour.

"Some days I don't think he has forgiven me. But divorce wasn't an option. For Dave. I'd felt like I should let him go. Let him find happiness elsewhere, with someone better—someone who wouldn't do what I had done. But he wouldn't hear of it. For your sake, Ella."

She reached over as if to pat my hand but then pulled back, tucking her fingers into a fist.

"Honestly, I've struggled since to forgive myself."

"Then, why do it? Why cheat? Why stay? Why?"

She looked at me, and I saw the same fear ripple through her soul that slid over mine. I shivered, clutching the edges of the blanket tighter in my hands.

"Because sometimes you don't act in your own best interests. Or rationally. Or with any thought other than to make the pain of the day-to-day stop."

I swallowed slowly, trying to get enough moisture in my throat to ask the next question. "You think I should forgive him? You think that Simon wasn't completely rational when he…"

Mum shook her head, her eyes tearing up again. "Sometimes,

we do things that we will regret for the rest of our lives. No matter what the final outcome."

CHAPTER FOURTEEN
Simon

Angelica hovered outside my hotel room door. I stopped midstride. The elevator started to close and I hurried forward, scowling at the young woman in her jersey sweater dress.

"This is a bit much. Don't you have something else to do?"

"Yes. I have lots of other things to do." She pressed those sleek black frames up her nose. "But right now, *you* are my priority."

"I don't think I like the sound of that."

"You shouldn't," she said with cheer.

"Let's get this over with. Why are you here?" I shoved my keycard into the lock. After I opened the door, I waved Angelica into the room.

"Seems like you haven't managed to get back with your wife."

"Thanks for pointing out the obvious." I tossed the keycard and my wallet on the desk, followed by my keys. "Anything else?"

"Um, you look like you haven't slept much."

I settled into the small love seat with a sigh, waving Angelica to the chair. "All true. On a positive note, I found out the child Ella's carrying—that she's struggling to carry—is most definitely mine. The doctor I met with also shared that the baby doesn't have Huntington's disease like my brother and father did."

"That must be a relief."

I dropped my head back against the unforgiving cushion. "You have no idea. I've watched what that disease does to people." I swallowed the sour taste of fear. "I'm not sure I could put a child, put Ella and Jeremiah through that kind of pain."

"Aren't we having a Superman complex today."

I cracked my eye open long enough to glare at Angelica, before closing it again. My tear-fest with Jeremiah at the park released some of the pent-up emotions but also caused my eyes to burn. Two weeks ago, I was high on the knowledge that fans packed out the arenas to hear me sing. Now, I desperately wanted to hold my wife and sleep more than three hours straight.

"Christmas is in three days."

I lifted my head and glared at Angelica again. "Right. Don't you have someone at home to share it with? Instead of butting in to my life further?"

She tipped her head to study me but I caught the faintest tremble of her lips. "No. I don't. As you know, my father's dead as is my mom. Breast cancer. Three years ago. My parents were both only children as am I." She spread her arms out. "This is as good as it gets for me at holidays. Hanging out with grouchy, troubled musicians."

I leaned forward and took Angelica's thin, cold hand in mine. "I'm sorry. I shouldn't have said that. I was cruel."

She pulled her hand from mine and stood. "Not intentionally, but that's what started this whole mess, hmm? So, what are you giving Ella? And Jeremiah?"

I dropped my linked hands between my spread knees. "I think Ella wants me to spend time with Miah. Build that relationship again. Prove that I won't leave her—or our son—make sure he knows he can count on me."

Angelica pursed her lips as she dipped her head. "Smart."

"But for El...I don't know."

Angelica leaned her hips against the small desk and waited. When had this young woman—a woman who only cared about my professional image—become my confidant? I blew out a breath and rolled my neck back on my shoulders.

Right.

Time to move forward. I needed a plan. A solid one that would help Ella understand the depths of my love for her and my intentions to remain faithful to my vows.

I stood suddenly as the idea torpedoed through my mind.

"Is there any way we can get Ella's students together? No, the whole school." I slammed my palms against the desk. "Yeah! All the teachers, the administrators and all the students?"

Angelica took off her glasses and began polishing them on a small square she pulled from her pocket. "What crazy idea ran into your mind?"

I tugged on my lip. "Definitely crazy. Probably stupid. Possibly embarrassing. For me. Not El. I won't do that to her."

Angelica settled her glasses back on her nose and picked up the hotel stationary and pen. "Let's have it."

CHAPTER FIFTEEN
Ella

Simon didn't show up the next day. I spent the morning hours on the settee in the parlor, watching snow fall in gentle puffs. By early afternoon, I moseyed back to my bedroom and read. I ate whatever my mother put in front of me. I napped. I talked to the baby and to Jeremiah. He even hugged me. Twice.

All in all, a relaxing day. Perfect, really.

I missed Simon.

Bugger the man. I wanted to yell at him. I wanted to kiss him. Mainly, I wanted his arms around my back, holding me tight and promising never to let go.

He never stopped by.

He did, however, drop off all my favorite sweets from a small bakery in Bath, something I found out only later as I'd still been sleeping at the time. Mum and I oohed and ahed over the fancy presentation while Jeremiah made short work of the truffles before heading upstairs to meet up with Mason and a few of his other friends to play on his Xbox, leaving Mum and I alone.

I stared down at the treat in front of me, then at the small curl of steam floating upward from my cup of tea. "I don't know what to think about our conversation yesterday."

Mum smiled, but it was filled with sadness. "I don't expect you to condone my actions. I don't."

"Where's Dad?" I asked.

Mum began to pick up the wrappers and the lunch plates. "Out."

"Where?"

"He didn't say."

I narrowed my eyes on her back. "Will he be here for Christmas?"

Mum turned around, her eyes shadowed. "Are you worried about that?"

I blew out a long breath. "Yes. I guess I am."

"Of course he'll be here."

"All right. Did Dad go off with Simon?"

Mum dried her hands on a dish towel and set it aside before resuming her seat at the table. "Yes. Your father said he'd be home this evening but not to hold dinner for him."

"Where did they go? Why? Dad's so angry with Simon right now."

"He is, true. Simon asked him. I don't know more than that, Ella. I'm sorry."

I frowned, my hands falling to my stomach in a protective gesture. More of my family couldn't fall apart. My breath shattered as I considered the possibility my parents might split up.

"You're sure you two are okay?"

Mum leaned down and pressed a soft kiss to my cheek. "No need to worry over us. Your father and I are better than we've been in years. Now, rest up." Mum handed me my Kindle and shooed me from the kitchen.

After settling onto the settee, I clicked on my e-reader, staring down at the words in front of me without seeing them.

I set my e-reader aside and turned to face the window, wishing I knew more about my father's day-jaunt.

Mostly, though, I wanted to stop trembling with the fear that Simon decided I wasn't worth the effort to woo once again.

CHAPTER SIXTEEN
Simon

My talk with Ella's father relieved none of my concerns. I'd brought him to the pub, explaining my idea over a lunch of fish and chips and lager and lime.

"Marsha said she overheard your conversation with that young woman." Dave pushed back his plate, tossing the white paper napkin on top.

"Angelica?"

"The young lady at the hospital."

"She's my…well, right now my crisis-management specialist, I guess. But she's my new point of contact at the studio." I wiped my hands on my napkin and took a long sip of my beer.

"Hmmm."

"What does that mean?" I asked.

"Seems like you've spent more time with that woman than with Ella."

"First off, Ella doesn't want to see me. Second, you don't want me near Ella."

Dave rubbed his hand down his chin. "It's not that, exactly."

"Oh?"

Dave wrapped his thick fingers around the pint glass. "Look, I appreciate the effort you're making with Jeremiah. He's a good boy and deserves to feel safe and loved."

"Couldn't agree more." I met my father-in-law's gaze, letting him see all the raw hurt I carried in my soul. "I don't want to leave Ella, Dave." I relaxed my fisted hands, smoothed them down my thighs. I cleared my throat. "I want to be the husband she deserves. The father my children need."

Dave glanced around the pub, his face holding the same level of consternation it had when Ella brought him to my first big international festival in Liverpool two years ago. "I understand numbers. Those make sense. This desire to create, to express yourself, seems like it just causes lots of selfishness."

I rubbed my palms over my cheeks. "I'm going to do right by my family. I'd like your blessing, of course, but I need to show Ella how much she means to me."

"Ella needs support. Emotional and financial."

I brought my gaze back up to his. "You're talking about Philip Wagner."

Dave shook his head. "No. I'm talking about my relationship with Marsha. She wanted to leave me, you know."

I clasped my hands together next to my half-filled plate and waited.

"She'd had an affair." He cleared his throat. "Took me years to get past it. Ella deserves better than I had. Than you've given her. If you can't do that for her, maybe it's best you just let things go. We'd love to have her home."

No way I could argue with that logic—Dave and Marsha made two trips a year while Ella usually made one trek back across the Atlantic. My parents were no longer alive, so Jeremiah needed this relationship with Ella's family. Unfortunately, the whole US continent and the Atlantic Ocean caused less closeness than any of us would have liked.

"I never meant for you to feel excluded from Ella's life."

Dave met my eye. "Distance did that. We never felt unwelcome in your home. Just limited by time and air fare."

"We'll have to do better—about traveling this way, then."

Dave's smile warmed even as he shook his head. "With an infant? And Jeremiah's select football schedule? And Ella's work and your touring schedule? I don't think we'll see more of any of you in person. But at least we now have that video call feature. It'll be good for Marsha to see the bub's steps and words and all that."

I chewed over that conversation, trying to wrap my head around my lack of attention to so many details. Sometimes, the living of life got in the way of seeing priorities.

"If Ella and I can work through this...I'll see to it that we put more effort into visiting."

"Appreciate the thought," Dave said, tossing back the last of his beer.

"There's one more thing." I hesitated. "I'd like you to bring Ella here, tomorrow. I plan to do a show. For her and for her school back home."

Dave settled back against the booth, hands over his middle. "Why would you do that?"

"I never would have sent divorce papers to Ella's school. I want to put the rumor mill there to rest. And." I sighed, rubbing the back of my neck. I raised my head and eyed him. Ella's always liked these small performances best. I thought...well, it's the best way to show her how much she means to me."

"New-fangled ideas on love," Dave grumbled.

"One more thing. I'd like this to be a surprise. For Ella."

Dave eyed the pub again, his expression dubious. He met my gaze. His pale-blue eyes softened more. "I get that you want to put this to rights, Simon. I appreciate that. I'll bring Ella. But you need to understand something, young man. She's cut clean to her core. This idea of yours might not be enough to heal that deep of a cut."

———◆———

Nerves skittered through my belly. I heaved a breath. My stomach refused to settle.

What if this crazy plan didn't work?

What if Ella couldn't leave the house to come to the pub or, worse, what if she did show up and didn't care?

I splayed my hands wide on the plastered wall, dropping my head between my shoulders as I stared down at the old wooden floor under my feet.

Stage fright, but worse. Because I wasn't performing for any of the people who'd see this show. I was laying my heart bare for Ella and had no idea how she'd respond.

After fifteen years of marriage, another two of dating, I'd thought I was long-past this point in my life: the fear of rejection, of not being able to read Ella's emotions or decipher her actions.

"Are you ready?" Angelica asked.

I flinched, yanked from my revelry. "You surprised me." I placed a hand over my galloping heart and muttered a curse. "No, I'm not sure I'm ready. I'm nervous. Everything's set, right?"

Angelica nodded, bouncing up and down on her small heels.

"Oh," she said. "A piece of news I thought you'd want to see." She tucked her agenda under her arm and pulled out her phone. After pulling up a screen, she handed the device to me. I squinted in the low light, trying to read the words.

I placed the phone back into Angelica's hand with care

because mine shook. "Monique dropped any further claims against me or the label?"

Angelica nodded, beaming up at me.

"You know her," I said. "She mentioned your history in that email." I pointed at the screen. Angelica waved her hand, her eyes dropping from mine.

"Irrelevant. All water under the bridge. The important detail is that Monique won't bother you again."

I swept Angelica up in my arms and hugged her tight. "Thanks. I still don't get why you're helping me but, right now, all the effort you've put in…it means a lot. If I can help you out, I'll be there."

Angelica patted her hair as she put more distance between us. "Oh, I'll be sure to take you up on that. Sooner rather than later." Her grin turned cheeky. "Right now, though? Why don't you get out there and do what you said you wanted to?"

I glanced over Angelica's head, craning my neck but unable to see most of the crowd. "Is Ella here?" I asked.

"She wasn't when I was out there."

Dave said he'd bring Ella, Jeremiah, and Marsha. I should have faith in his word, but…after hearing about his and Marsha's problems, I wasn't as keen to believe in him as I'd hoped to be.

I nodded, but my stomach tightened and my throat ached. Not a good placed to be as a singer. I snagged a bottle of water and chugged it.

I grabbed my guitar and walked out onto the small stage. Just me, my guitar, a stool, and a microphone. Talk about a return to the basics.

But this needed to happen, and I needed to do this—for me, for Ella, and for the world.

I settled onto the stool and took a moment to suck in another deep belly breath of air, bending over my guitar to look like I was tuning the already tuned instrument. After releasing the breath slowly, I raised my head and smiled. My gaze flicked through the audience and I sought the only pair of eyes that mattered—two sets, actually. I landed on Philip, whose arms remained crossed over his chest, a slight scowl marring his brow. He'd positioned himself next to a thick beam. Dave sat on the other side, rheumy eyes focused on me. Marsha sat beside him, her purse clutched in her hands.

No sign of Jeremiah or Ella.

Well. So much for hope. Now, I'd have to focus on the message—one I hoped her father relayed to her.

"Thanks for coming out tonight. Christmas Eve. You all having a good one?"

The crowd cheered. Some of them raised pint glasses. None of them understood the war battling in my chest. None except maybe Philip, and it wasn't like he wanted me to succeed.

"Let's play a few tunes. Whatcha say?"

The crowd roared its approval, and I smiled. But I wasn't in to the performance. At all. These were motions to go through, not the excitement or the adrenaline rush that typically surrounded a performance.

I wanted Ella here.

I wanted Ella. Period.

She made her point though. She wasn't ready to forgive me. Maybe she couldn't.

Maybe I should simply cut my losses, tuck my tail, and run like Dave had suggested.

But first I had fans to please. And if I'd learned anything over the years, it was how to perform for the crowd.

Every song on my list tonight I'd written for Ella or Jeremiah. I started with the song I used to sing to Ella's belly when she was pregnant with Miah. My lips quirked up when I remembered how I'd get close to her tummy and watch, fascinated, as the mound shifted with our son's movements. When I stopped singing he'd stop moving.

"Sing another," Ella would say, rubbing her hands up and down her bump. "He dances when you sing."

I missed those moments. I wanted them again, with our daughter. With Ella.

I finished the song on a bit of a sigh. Not ideal for a singer, but this performance meant more to me than critical reviews.

I strummed out the second song in my set, then a third. But the fourth, my nausea dissipated, but so did my faith that music—my willpower, even Angelica's awesome organizational abilities—would fix what I broke.

"So, I have just a couple more songs this evening. I hope you all there in Seattle are enjoying this session as much as the crew here."

I'd chosen not to broadcast back a video of the student body packed into the gymnasium at Ella's school, deciding that would be more than my shaky nerves could handle. Angelica gave me the thumbs up, but her mouth remained pinched.

Better make this one count. Those kids needed to know how special Ella was to me—whatever came of our relationship.

"Most of you students there at Franklin High know my wife simply as your choral teacher. But I wanted to tell you a story about the day we met. There's a sport here in England called cricket." The raucous crowd in the pub bellowed and stomped their feet.

"I'd never played before, being American and into baseball, but I was lucky enough to have a full semester at Cambridge. I decided to learn all things British, so I signed up for what we Americans call a rec league. First person onto the field was this petite young woman with the most amazing eyes. She wore the cricket whites better than any of her teammates."

I winked at the crowd here, who'd lowered their glasses and leaned forward, hanging on my every word.

"She walloped me in cricket and then she landed me flat on my butt when she sang some British battle song."

Such a beautiful voice to go along with those beautiful eyes. I smiled at the memory of her first glance in my direction—her eyes widened before a small smile lifted her lips. A blush stained her fair, rounded cheeks. I'd never understood the term heart-shaped face until Ella.

Lord, she was lovely with those bright eyes, soft pink lips and brown hair tumbling over narrow shoulders all the way to her tiny waist.

"I fell in love with her over the next month of cricket games and study sessions and…" Never mind what else. Ella's students didn't need to hear those details. "I asked her to visit me before I had to fly home to Seattle. She did, and it turned into more. She chose to finish her senior year at Northern. We've been together, singing, raising our son since."

I cleared my throat and leaned in closer to the microphone. "There's no one I'd rather spend the rest of my life with. There's no one I'll ever enjoy singing with as much. So, whatever you've heard in the media or think you know from rumors at school, I want to put all that to rest."

Now the hard part. I met Philip's eyes, then Dave's. He hadn't given me his blessing—I'm sure he'd withhold opinion for a while longer—but he did seem to want Ella happy. I hoped I could be the one to bring a smile to her face again.

"Ella, I love you more today than the day I married you. I'll love you even more when I die. Thank you for taking this journey with me. I never realized how hard it must have been to leave your home, your family, when I asked you to make a life with me. But you did because you're strong and resourceful. And you'll always be the better cricket player."

I paused, my throat clogged by the lump of emotion.

"And thank you twice over for our incredible children."

There was a soft snuffle from the crowd, but I didn't care. The words I'd said were meant for one set of ears—ears not here to listen to what I was telling her.

With a deep breath, I focused on the bartender across the large pub. I strummed out the opening chords of the song I'd written for Ella for our honeymoon. I hadn't sung this one in public ever.

Ella asked me to keep the song private—between us—and I had, always. But I hoped she understood I was doing this to show just how much I did love her. Because this tune was a bit too soft, a bit too sweet even for my ballad-laden albums.

As the lyrics swirled through my head, my chest constricted. Damn. We'd been so in love. So sure of ourselves, and our futures.

Look at us now.

I closed my eyes, my fingers sliding up and down the strings, and let my memories—all our years together—take over.

I finished the song and bowed my head, overcome by what I'd lost.

No. Worse.

I'd held the most amazing love in my hands, pressed her body close to mine for years. And I'd chosen to throw her—us—away.

CHAPTER SEVENTEEN
Ella

I pressed my hand to my lips, my breath stuttering in short pants over my cold fingertips.

Philip looked down at me, where I'd settled in a chair behind the thick wooden beam. His eyes twinkled with a bit of the mischief I used to adore. But it was tempered by another emotion.

"He doesn't know you're here. He said that, did that, because he wanted to make the situation right."

Jeremiah leaned his head against my shoulder, and I wrapped my arm around his neck. Though he wouldn't like it, I pressed a kiss to his hair, which he tolerated because he must understand my need for closeness.

"I've always cared for you, Ella."

Jeremiah raised his head, eyes narrowed, mouth set.

Philip smiled again, raising his hands to head off whatever Jeremiah wanted to say.

"But Simon adores you. Truly. Deeply. Just so you know, I've never felt *that* deep a connection with anyone."

"I know."

Philip smiled again, and that other emotion shone brighter. Regret. No, acceptance. Philip accepted that Simon loved me deeper, truer than he ever had—or could.

"You always were the smartest woman in any room, El Bel." He leaned in and squeezed my fingers. "I hope you find every bit of love you deserve."

Before Jeremiah blinked again, Philip leaned back in his chair and crossed his arms over his chest, face impassive as he stared at

Simon pouring out his heart.

I laid my head on the table as Simon began to play the song he wrote for me one day as we toured our way through Sonoma Valley. We honeymooned during Labor Day weekend, the days full of warm September sun, rich California cabernet, love-making, and song. We'd always sung together.

Simon hadn't sung to me—only me—in over a year.

Jeremiah huffed out a breath that almost seemed like a sob. "He's trying, Mom."

"I hear that, son."

I let the simple chords, the soft croon of Simon's voice wash over me, soothing my abraded heart. *This* was what I'd missed: His making music for the emotion behind it. Because the song must find voice.

I glanced over at my father, who'd wrapped an arm around my mum. She rested her head against his shoulder, her fingers clutched over his.

They fought for their relationship. Thinking back, I couldn't remember a time in my life when I didn't feel love from my parents. For me, of course, but also for each other.

Rough patches happened, even in the best of relationships. Hadn't I seen that before? Not just in my parents' but in my colleagues, and in Lia's and Asher's.

I peeked around the corner just in time to see Simon scan the room, his eyes roving hungrily before he bowed his head in disappointment.

"Now for my last song. It's brand-new. Not one I intended to play, but…" He trailed off. "Sometimes life changes. Sometimes you fall down." He blew out a breath. "And sometimes, you take down the people you care about most in the process."

The chords were more complex—a testament to his growth as a musician. The minor chords settled over me. Simon liked to play with them—push them as far as he could go while remaining upbeat. This melody teetered on the edge of complete heartbreak.

And then he began to sing.

A cloud passed before the sun,
On that day when we fell down
Now, I miss your eyes and your smile
I want to ask you just to sit awhile
But the dark consumes me as the clouds rolled in
On the day when we fell down.

I didn't catch the rest of the words. My heart hammered to loud.

His face…the way his lips twisted and his eyes beseeched…he hurt, too.

As much as I did.

Why hadn't I seen that?

I didn't want to see it.

The last note faded, the crowd hooted and hollered, clearly unaware of how much of his soul Simon left in their ears tonight.

"Thanks for coming. Have a great holiday."

Simon's shoulders heaved and he lifted his left hand, standing fast enough to make his stool screech across the wooden stage. He strode forward, not even acknowledging the ear-splitting applause.

I stood, too. My legs wobbled a bit, and I blinked back the strange black globs floating through my vision.

"Simon."

He kept walking. Almost to the door. His shoulders rose

again, as if he was breaking down.

"Simon," I cried, hurrying forward. I scuttled around a rowdy group of university boys and another older set of men who hooted as I bounded past.

He reached the door. His hand grasped the knob.

"Simon."

He disappeared through the door.

It shut with a deep resonate thud.

Like he'd just sealed our fate.

No. *No*. He couldn't be gone.

CHAPTER EIGHTEEN
Simon

I finished the set.

I said some final words and waved. I strode off the stage and didn't look back. I shoved my guitar into its case and snapped the locks before grabbing my coat. Shoving my arms into the sleeves, I picked up my guitar case and snagged my car keys.

"Where are you running off to?" Angelica said, breathless, her eyes alight.

"Home." I paused, my fingers going numb. Except I didn't know where that was anymore. I'd given up the right to my house in Seattle when I visited my lawyer.

Shit. This was hard.

"Don't you want to know how the simulcast was received?"

"No."

I headed across the narrow, wood-paneled room we'd used as a staging area for my minimal gear. I grabbed a water and downed it in a few thirsty gulps. As soon as I threw the bottle in the trash can, I strode toward the far side of the room with a door that led outside.

"Not even if I tell you more than three million people watched live? And the comments on that last song…my goodness, Simon. I have shivers."

"Don't care. I performed tonight for one…two people. No one else mattered."

I reached the door. My hand gripped the cold knob. I turned it, opening it to walk out into the rest of my lonely life.

Her voice reached me, warming my insides even as the cold

blast of wet English winter slapped my face.

"I bloody well hope I'm one of the two."

I whirled back, my guitar case sliding from my fingers, my throat clogged with a thick, deep emotion. The bitter cold wafted through the door, causing me to shiver. I stepped back into the room, closer my wife.

"Ella."

She stepped forward, too, and uncertainty boiled through the depths of her lovely eyes. "Was I? One of the people you played for tonight."

Desperate though I was to touch her, I fisted my hand. I couldn't help moving deeper into the room where she hovered by the door leading into the pub. As if she might need to make an escape. From me.

How could I go the rest of my life and not touch Ella? Not cradle her cheek in my palm? How would I survive without the ability to run my hand down her spine and cup her derriere, dragging her closer, then closer still?

Why had I listened to other people when I knew, always understood that Ella was my love, my rock, my greatest passion?

Pain lanced its way through my chest. No way I could ever, ever recover from this blow.

"You're the most important person. And Jeremiah."

Ella crossed her arms over her chest, which forced her small bump into prominence. "What about the baby? Ready to claim her yet?"

I shoved the heels of my hands against my eyes, trying to force the moisture back inside me. If I started crying, the tears would wipe me out.

"I love her, too. I can't wait to meet her and hold her and…" The tears streamed down my face. I didn't bother to wipe them away. More would follow. "I don't want to miss a moment of her life. If I could get out of my contract, I would."

Ella cocked her head to the side. Her hair slid across her shoulder, and I wanted to run my hand over its silky weight. My fists tightened.

"The last time you cried was at your brother's funeral."

I grumbled a little. "I'm not much for this kind of emotion."

"Did you mean that? Getting out of your contract?" Ella's voice remained careful, her eyes watchful. I hated the chasm I'd created between us.

This time, I snorted with rueful humor. "Asher told me fame and money weren't all that great. I thought he was blasé—I mean, he's a freaking legend with plenty of money in the bank to do whatever he wants." I couldn't help it. I had to step closer, to smell her subtle scent—the lavender she kept in the coat closet and in her clothes drawers.

Ella plucked a tissue from her pocket and handed it to me. I wiped my wet cheeks and nose before shoving the soggy cotton into my pocket. I stiffened my shoulders and met her gaze. "But what I didn't understand was I already had *everything* I needed and more than I deserved."

I stretched my hand out, my finger trembling as I ran the very tips down her cheek. Her eyes closed and a pained expression crossed her face.

"I messed up. I know it. I can't go back and change it. All I can hope for is that you can forgive me. That you'll let me prove how much you mean to me."

The pause between us grew. I couldn't take it. If she planned to tell me to get lost, I needed one last connection. One last kiss to keep me warm and yearning for the rest of my lonely, dark days.

I leaned in, my head tilting right as she tipped her chin, dipping her forehead to the left. This, at least, was familiar. The shock of her lips zinged through me. Perfect. But different. Hers tasted of lemonade and a hint of ginger. I rubbed mine over hers, licking at the corners before sealing our mouths together. She clutched my coat low at my waist just above the rear pockets of my jeans. I moaned, desperate for her mouth, for her taste, for her love.

With a tremulous noise, Ella opened for me. I pressed my tongue inside, my right hand cupping her head as I delved in, then again and again, seeking the succor Ella had always provided.

Her tongue touched mine with a tentativeness that brought a growl to my throat. I didn't want Ella timid. I wanted her vibrant and strong and the woman I'd fallen in love with.

I pulled her tighter to my chest, my need for oxygen making me light-headed, but I didn't release her.

Not until light flutters skittered across my belly. I pulled back, and her hands fell to her sides. My eyes widened with the longing to feel my daughter move again.

She did. Barely more than the lightest drift of wind. But I felt her. I dropped to my knees, my lips pressed to Ella's stomach, my arms wrapped as tight as I dared around Ella's hips.

"Hi, baby. I'm your daddy. I can't wait to meet you."

The baby kicked again, and I chuckled as I rubbed my cheek against Ella's belly. She dropped her hands into my hair, connecting to me.

"But maybe slow down on giving your mom such a hard time. We got lots of years to worry over you, okay?"

Ella made a strangled noise, her fingertips touching her lips, her eyes filling with tears.

"What? What is it?" I asked. My anxiety spiked. "Do you feel okay?"

She met my gaze, tears leaking from the corners of her eyes. "I can't do this alone. I don't want to raise this girl without you."

I pulled her tight to my chest, my throat working as another bout of emotion brimmed there. "You don't have to. I'll never ask that of you. I promise."

I glanced up at the soft sound across the room. I caught a glimpse of Jeremiah's grin and Angelica's back before the door that led into the pub clicked shut.

CHAPTER NINETEEN
Ella

I launched myself forward, hurtling too fast, but Simon caught me. As he had that first night of our honeymoon in Sonoma when I leapt from halfway down the staircase. As he had when I miscarried seven years ago.

But this embrace was gentle, his arms absorbing my weight as he maneuvered my slight belly so it was cradled against his stomach.

His nose found its spot in the curve of my neck and we both exhaled in a rush.

"Ella. Shit, El, I've missed you."

"Simon." I pulled him tighter to me, needing his strength, his warmth. Needing him.

I soaked up Simon's unique scent, the strength of the tendon and sinew that cradled me with such care. The soft rasp of his voice as he whispered his sorrow, his love into my skin.

———————

We stayed there, in that drafty back room in the pub, wrapped around each other for much longer.

Finally, Simon pulled back, his eyes red-rimmed. "You need to get off your feet. Let me take you home."

"Back to your hotel," I said.

Simon shook his head. "Tomorrow's Christmas. We're going to your parents'. That is." He dropped his gaze, suddenly unsure. "Do you think they'll let me stay?"

I nodded, unable to speak around the lump in my throat.

Simon grabbed my hand, wrapping his much larger one around my fingers. He bent enough to grasp his guitar case and led me out into the late evening. Snow drifted in large, lacey flakes.

"A Christmas snow," I said with a smile.

Simon tightened his grip. "Excellent. Miah and I can have a sledding rematch."

Simon opened my car door. I glanced around, shocked Simon's was one of the only vehicles in the lot.

Angelica popped up from a nice SUV nearby. "Jeremiah went home with your parents about an hour ago," she said. "If you're heading back with Ella for the night, I can pick up your luggage and deliver it to you tomorrow."

Angelica looked between the two of us, shivering slightly as the snow blew down the neck of her cashmere sweater.

Simon looked down at me, letting me know without words it was my choice.

"Yes, that's lovely," I said. "Thanks."

"Angelica?" Simon said. "What are your plans for tomorrow?"

Angelica shrugged. "I told you—I don't really have anyone to celebrate with."

"You most certainly do," I said. "You'll have the day with us."

"I don't want to impose," Angelica said, rubbing her hands up and down her arms.

"That's no trouble a'tall," I said. "My mum loves to cook. There'll be plenty."

Angelica's smile lit up her face and the air between us, causing me to gasp in delight.

"I'd really like that," she said in a soft voice.

"Tomorrow, then," Simon said. "Thank you for all the help." He turned toward me, ready to assist me into my seat.

"It's my job," Angelica said in that gratingly cheerful voice.

Simon closed his eyes for a moment before he met mine. "She's probably not joking."

I choked back a laugh and settled into my seat with a sigh.

My body ached with exhaustion, but my mind drifted, at peace for the first time in months.

I turned my head to look at my husband when he slid into his seat, shivering a little at the dropped temperature.

"I've missed you," I said.

He picked up my hand and pressed a kiss to my glove-covered palm, closing my fingers over the promise he'd made there.

"I've been desperate for you."

I smiled as I closed my eyes.

———◆———

The car stopped, and I blinked with groggy intent.

"Where are we?"

"Your parents' house."

"I fell asleep."

"Just ten minutes."

I made a movement to open the car door, but Simon placed his hand on my thigh. I shivered.

"Shh," Simon whispered. "I'll get you."

He pulled me from the car, and I snuggled tight against his chest. "Promise you won't leave me," I murmured.

He kissed the top of my head. "I promise."

After locking my parents' back door, he climbed the stairs and settled me in the bed. He took off my shoes and pulled off my jeans before covering me with the sheet and blankets.

I rolled over and pressed my body to his. "Love me, Simon."

His lips slid up my jaw to my lips. Our lips and arms clung to each other—our limbs a tangle. I ran my hands back up to his hair and giggled when the leather of my gloves caught in the strands. I pulled them off with my teeth.

They fell to the bed as I tunneled my fingers back into his hair. Simon continued his assault on my jawline and throat. I hummed, enjoying the leashed urgency in his touch.

"I don't want to hurt you, Ella. Neither you nor the baby."

"You won't."

I moved my hands to his abdominals, sliding my palms up his stomach and chest. He heaved a breath, his eyes meeting mine. The desire there in those hazel depths flared brighter—as did his love.

I needed that look, the soft touch of his lips and finger tips.

"Don't make me wait," I whispered. "I need you."

"I need you, too, El."

He continued to touch, caress me. His lips followed his fingers across my heated, flushed flesh until I ached for him, writhing and clenching my jaw to keep silent. With careful hands, Simon removed the rest of my clothes. He stood, yanking off his shirt, pants and underwear with quick movements. He inhaled sharply, clearly trying to get himself under control, before he crawled back into the bed, kissing my shoulder, then down the slope of my breast.

His hands fitted to my ribs, holding me close as he licked and nipped his way, murmuring love words. My chest heaved and my hands fisted in the sheet.

On and on, he worshipped my body, bringing me close but never letting me fall over the peak. I scrabbled for purchase—to keep my world right as it narrowed to his hands, lips, tongue, skin.

"I need you," I murmured.

"You have me," he said as he entered my body.

I heaved a sob, clutching him tighter.

"Simon."

"I'm here. I'm right here with you, Ella."

He was. He held me as he loved me with gentle insistence. I strained toward him, trying to alleviate the tight coil of desire building.

On the next thrust, my release slammed into me. Simon pressed his lips to mine, swallowing my cry. He slid out, in, grunted as his body tensed with his orgasm. We slid, boneless, and breathing hard, back to the sheets.

He pulled both my hands up to his mouth and pressed firm kisses to my knuckles.

"I love you, Ella. God, I love you. Being away from you slays me."

"I love you, too." I yawned wide enough to pop my jaw. I winced.

Simon chuckled. He climbed from the bed and padded naked to the en suite bathroom. I enjoyed the way the moonlight filled his dips in shadows, highlighting the ridges of muscle he worked hard to maintain.

He returned with a cloth and insisted on cleaning me. After returning the cloth to the bathroom, he brought me my flannel pajama pants and candy cane tee. I slid into them, a decadence warming my blood at my lack of panties. Simon pulled back on his boxer briefs and returned to the bed. He wrapped his arms around my waist, tucking my back to his chest.

We both shivered as the cool air from the room dissipated, replaced by our body heat. I snuggled in tighter, curling into the ball I preferred to sleep in these days.

"Promise you won't hurt me," I whispered.

Oh, Ella. I'll move mountains to keep you from being hurt again."

Christmas Day proved low-key and much happier than I'd anticipated.

Angelica showed up midmorning with Simon's bags. Jeremiah's eyes sparked to life when he saw them, his eyes brimming with hope when they raised to mine.

"I love your father," I said as Jeremiah stepped forward, settling next to me on the settee. "And he says he loves me."

Simon came and sat on my other side, picking up my hand. "I do. You, too, Jeremiah." His fingers drifted over the slight rounding of my belly. "And this little peanut."

"What does this mean?" Jeremiah asked, his voice cracking.

I opened my mouth, but no words came out. I glanced up at Simon, not wanting to speak for him—unsure where we went from here.

"Glad you asked," Simon said, voice brisk.

He squeezed my fingers before laying my hand back in my lap. He rose and went over to his bag where he pulled out a few presents. He settled them on the coffee table in front of me and his eyes darted to my parents, then Angelica's. She nodded.

He took a deep breath and turned back to me.

"So, I've had some time to think about what I want." He cleared his throat. "I'm hopeful that it's what you want, too, Ella, but we'll need to talk it through. Compromise to make sure you're both happy."

Simon's tentativeness caused my heart to ache, but he needed to understand what his sole focus on his career did to our family.

He cleared his throat and glanced back at Angelica. She rolled her eyes and settled onto the large, tufted foot stool in front of my parents, who'd taken the overstuffed love seat.

"You make the best tea, Mrs. Browning."

"Thank you, dear," Mum replied. "So glad you could join us."

Simon swiped his hands down his jeans. "Erm, so…I can't coach your soccer team this year, not with my current commitments." He picked up a thin present and handed it to Jeremiah. "But I did talk to your coach and he helped me work out the details on this. I…I hope you like it. All of you."

Jeremiah ripped open the wrapping and gaped at the paper inside. "I get to work with…he's one of the most famous soccer legends in England…he's going to have a clinic here?"

Simon nodded, pulling a pamphlet from the stack of papers and handing it to me. "If…if it's okay, I thought, well, since it's hard for your parents to get to us as often as they'd like, and with the baby, you might want some help for when I can't be around…Angelica and I worked out my schedule for next summer so I can stick closer to you all here in England with some short trips, a couple of overnights onto the continent. That way, you get time with your folks, Ella, and they can spend time with all three of you, but we're together more."

"I thought it a marvelous idea," my father put in, smiling. "He asked me the other day before his concert." Dad rubbed at a spot behind his ear. "Seemed a way to keep everyone happier." He trailed off, turning to look at my mum, who patted his hand and beamed at him.

Simon sat next to me, showing me the dates. "Jeremiah can do the whole two-month course here. It doesn't start until end of June, which will give you time to wrap up your classroom and grading and everything—if you go back to work after the baby."

"I plan to stay home with her."

Simon's smile grew. "That'll give us more flexibility as to when we come then. I didn't make any reservations—I thought you'd want to decide on dates." His cheeks reddened. "Um, that's if you're okay with us spending the summer here."

"This will work for his touring schedule, Angelica?" I mightn't love Simon's newest career, but he did, and I needed to find a way forward that would best accommodate all of us.

"When he told me the idea, I started working with our team to rearrange a few things. It'll totally work and should help build his international following. Jon's on board." Angelica smiled at me. "We only had to schedule three overnights between July and September 1."

"Thank you," I said, a bit overwhelmed.

Angelica raised her tea in salute.

I turned to Simon and cupped his cheek. "And thank you… for understanding…for wanting family time."

"You're the most important people in my life." Simon pressed a soft kiss to my lips. His arms wrapped around me with warm insistence. This was what I'd missed. This was what I'd craved.

"I love happy endings," Angelica said, clasping her hands under her chin. She looked so young, and, for the first time since I met her, truly happy herself.

I turned my head so that I could meet Simon's warm gaze. The steady, patient light was back in his eyes. "I love you, Ella. I always have. And, I promise, I vow, I always will."

I blinked back the tears and cleared my throat. "I love you, too, Simon. So much. So damn much."

"Okay, too much sweetness," Angelica said on a sigh. "Enjoy your sappy moment. Jeremiah and I are going to the park. I must try out these sleds Simon bought. We'll catch you later!"

Jeremiah ran up and slammed into his father's side, wrapping his arms around both of us briefly, needing the reassurance that all was right in his world once again. He'd buried his nose in Simon's neck but jumped, as did Simon, when the baby kicked. Hard.

"Blimey. I think she broke my bladder with that one," I gasped.

"My sister's not messing around." Jeremiah giggled. "See you soon, baby." He patted my belly, and then he trotted off, accepting the hand Angelica held out to him. Caught in such a strange, magical place between young man and child, Jeremiah owned my heart. Glancing up at Simon who looked after our son with much the same expression I must be wearing, my chest warmed. Oh, this man. He held my happiness in his hands.

Now, after nearly breaking it—breaking me—he reconfirmed his commitment to our family.

My trust wouldn't return as quickly as either of us would like, but, over time, I hoped—no, I knew, I'd learn Simon meant what he said.

We stood there for another long moment, enjoying the spring's soft sun and the warmth from each other.

"Let's take a little walk," Simon said. "If you're up for it."

"Sure," I said.

"Be careful, poppet," Mum said. She brought me my coat, hat, scarf, and gloves. Simon ran upstairs to grab all his winter gear. My father waylaid him in the hall when he galloped down the stairs.

"I'm glad you two are working out your worries," Mum said, fussing over my zipper.

"We're trying."

She took a deep breath and laid her hands on my shoulders. "I've never had the love you two share." She dipped her chin and smiled. "Don't get me wrong. Your father and I love each other. But you and Simon." She sighed. "He's part of your very soul."

I leaned forward and pressed a kiss to her cheek. "I just hope I'm always a part of his."

——◆——

"Will you miss the bigger stadiums?" I asked as we meandered down the street. More snow fell in a soft, slow dance. "I never meant for you to give up performing, to quit your dream—"

He stopped on the sidewalk and turned toward me, his eyes searching mine. "I'm not quitting my dream. Like us, my dreams evolved."

116

I waited, wanting to hear more, needing the reassurance he could give me.

"Ah, El. I can't tell you how angry I am with myself. I already had everything I needed in you and Miah." He fumbled to grab both my gloved hands. "I nearly threw it away to perform for bigger crowds—that's all it is, really, a matter of scale. And the performing has never been as fulfilling as my life with you."

"I don't want you to resent me." I let go of his hands to spread out my arms. "Us." The baby kicked, and I winced. Simon grabbed my elbow. "My body doesn't seem as mobile as it was when I was pregnant with Jeremiah."

"Twelve years more wear and tear." Simon deadpanned as I made a half-hearted attempt to smack his arm—the only part of him I could reach. "For me, too, El. Me, too. But you know what doesn't change?" he asked.

He touched the corners of my eyes, his own gaze following his movement. He swept his fingertips up, gently, toward my brows and winged his fingers across them. "Your eyes. The love in them. The understanding that, yeah, I can be a selfish bastard, but I don't mean it." His lips quirked up. "At least not most of the time."

His fingers trailed down to my lips and he leaned forward, filling my vision. "And the connection in our kisses. I broke something vital when I didn't listen to your fears and insecurities, but I can still taste your caring, still feel the give in your soft lips. I'll listen better."

My breath shattered as he finished leaning in, fusing his mouth to mine. The touch was gentle, soft.

Just what I needed.

"I will, too." I fumbled for his hand, squeezing his gloved fingers. "I'm sorry. For not trusting enough."

"You have nothing to apologize for. We simply need to communicate better. And that starts with me being around more."

He turned as he heard Jeremiah's excited yell.

"Let's head back," Simon suggested.

"He wants to open the rest of his gifts, I'm sure."

Simon's arm wrapped around my waist. "Hope you got him something good."

"Nothing as good as your gift." I laughed. "He's over the moon."

Simon stopped. His face settling in stark lines. "I didn't know what to get you."

I reached up and touched his cheek, luxuriating in my right to do so as much as in the warmth that filtered through my glove.

"I have you."

He smiled, pressing a kiss to my gloved palm. "Always."

I began walking again, and Simon fell in step beside me, pulling me out of Jeremiah's way as our son made a mad dash toward the house.

"So, what else did you get me?" I asked, curious.

"Besides my undying love and affection?" Simon helped me up the two steps. He shrugged "Jewelry."

I grinned. "I'm sure I'll like it. But I'd rather have you. This. Us."

Simon placed my hand over his heart. My fingers curled toward the strong pulse as I raised my gaze to his.

"I promise."

EPILOGUE
Simon

Five Months Later

I touched the perfect, pink fingers and ran my hand up her plump arm.

"She's gorgeous," I murmured.

"She is."

"Did you settle on a name?" I asked, almost too enraptured to look up. My daughter. I held my baby girl in my arm.

"Well…"

My gaze rose to meet Ella's. She leaned back against the pillow, exhausted and glowing. Her cheeks were still thin, but they radiated with health, and her eyes remained bright as she smiled at us.

"You paint quite the picture there, Mr. Dorsey. You holding that precious girl."

I pressed a soft kiss to the pulse point on the top of her head. "She brings out my snuggler."

"As long as you save some for me."

My smile turned more heated. "Oh, that's a given." I cuddled my daughter closer. "So. Name."

Ella settled farther into her pillow. "I know it's May, but I wanted to name her something to remind me of our Christmas."

I nodded, my pulse pounding as it did each time she brought up that time. Not that Ella ever took advantage of my guilt—that was all on me.

"What do you think of Celyn?" She plucked at the blanket over her knee.

"That sounds…Irish?"

"Welsh. For Mum's heritage. It means Holly. A bit of a nod to our trials but purely her own."

"It's lovely. Like you." I leaned down and pressed a kiss to Celyn's plump cheek. "Celyn Dorsey."

"Celyn *Angelica* Dorsey."

My smile widened. Ella answered it and soon we both laughed.

"She's on her way," I said. "She was beside herself that her trip to LA took longer than expected."

Angelica might be my A&R director, but Ella treated her like a long-lost sister. The two of them bent their heads together, and whispered over ways to fix the world—and me—often.

My relationship with Ella strengthened each day because I'd kept my promise. When I had to tour, I called her at least twice to hear about her day and Jeremiah's. Angelica ensured me the time and privacy to do so.

Yep, Angelica was a godsend. And a good friend.

"Celyn Angelica. Between her and your mother, you have some strong ladies to live up to." I leaned in closer to my drowsy daughter. "But don't worry," I whispered. "I'm going to help you become just as mighty as they are."

"Too right," Ella whispered as she snuggled into the bed. Both she and Celyn blinked once, twice, before their eyes slid shut.

My girls.

I turned when the door opened. Jeremiah peeked his head in, eyebrows up in question. Ella's parents, Lia, Asher, and Mason all filed into the room after him.

I dipped my head at Lia, who smiled back. That relationship

remained a work in progress. Lia worried over my next bout of diva-hood, as she called it. Given my track record, I couldn't complain.

"We named her Celyn. Celyn Angelica."

Jeremiah grinned as he reached for the baby. My heart stuttered again as I looked at my gangly, tall-as-me teenage son with his floppy hair and soft, sweet smile holding his baby sister.

"Hey, Celyn. I got lots to teach you. But don't worry. I learned a few things." Jeremiah gave me a side-eye. "The most important thing I'll ever do is love you, just as you are."

I let out a sigh, a bit more of the regret and shame sliding from my body. Ella and I worked toward recovering our previous intimacy. She more than met me each day.

I was profoundly grateful to be here, in this room, with my greatest loves and our extended family.

And I would never, ever take these moments for granted.

ACKNOWLEDGMENTS

As always, thank you, Chris. Your unwavering support and love shine through in all you do for the kids and me. I couldn't ask for a better man, and I'm thrilled to wake up with you each day.

To my family, thank you for your patience with my dream—and letting me hang out in my head *way* too often.

LERA ladies and gentlemen, thank you for being so supportive, for making me love writing again, and for sharing your knowledge so freely. You are the best.

To my AuthorLab writing pals: You keep me on task and keep me motivated. I love your commitment and passion. I love reading your posts and stories. And I love how diverse our group is.

To Deb, thank you for seeing the big picture—and making sure I see it, too.

To Nicole, thank you for the advice on Seattle, and for generally being awesome.

To my Divas, especially Jane—you kicked ass with the eARC's and I can never thank you enough.

To Clarissa, once again the cover is gorgeous. I love working with you.

And to my readers and reviewers. Thank you for your time. It's precious, and I'm so, so glad you spent some of it with me.

ABOUT THE AUTHOR

With a degree in international marketing and a varied career path that includes content management for a web firm, marketing direction for a high-profile sports agency, and a two-year stint with a renowned literary agency, Alexa Padgett has returned to her first love: writing fiction.

Alexa spent a good part of her youth traveling. From Budapest to Belize, Calgary to Coober Pedy, she soaked in the myriad smells, sounds, and feels of these gorgeous places, wishing she could live in them all—at least for a while. And she does in her books.

She lives in New Mexico with her husband, children, and Great Pyrenees pup, Ash. When not writing, schlepping, or volunteering, she can be found in her tiny kitchen, channeling her inner Barefoot Contessa.

Turn the page for a sneak peek at Chapter one of A Moonlit Serenade, the final novel in the Seattle Sound series.

CHAPTER ONE
Ryn

"I'm supposed to meet with Ryn Hudson. You know, the songwriter."

"That's me," I said, looking up. Sweet jelly jiggles. I tried to pry my eyes away from those striking hazel eyes, the crooked brown brows, but I couldn't. His was the face of an angel—until panic flamed in his eyes and he lost all the color behind his sexy tan.

"No way. No." He even stumbled back. Like my studio was some type of horror show.

"Excuse me?" I said, hands dropping to my hips. Good thing my guitar was hooked around my neck by its strap. Otherwise, four thousand dollars' worth of handmade Taylor would be on the ground, dented, possibly broken.

"Ryn's a songwriter. A *musician*," he stressed the last word, his accent was strong. Not British, I didn't think. Unless it was Cockney. But he didn't sound like Adele, the only person whose voice I'd ever heard with that accent.

"I'm aware of what I am. Thank you very much."

"But you...you're playing chords for babies."

I glanced around my class, shocked to see all ten moms and their kids staring, just as awestruck by the man as I'd been moments before. Before he ticked me off.

"That's what we do. Play songs for the kids so they learn about pitch and rhythm. Well, in this case, we played 'Jingle Bells' because the song rocks, and it's close to Christmas."

"Oh," Helena moaned. "I think I'm going to die. I knew I should've combed my hair."

I glanced over at her, nonplussed by her drama. Her daughter Ilona sucked on her pacifier in slow, deep pulls, eyes lowered to dangerous, prenap-time levels.

"You're Jake Etsam," Stephani yelped. I didn't appreciate the predatory look in her eyes when she glanced at the angel-man. He'd asked for *me*. Ergo, he was mine.

Whoa. Hold the shaky eggs. Where had that thought come from?

"Oops, Kendall had a little problem there, Steph," I said, not trying to hide the laughter from my voice.

Stephani half moaned, half shrieked as Kendall upchucked more of her milk straight down Steph's low-cut, clingy top, her face as red as the poinsettias I'd placed on the top shelves of the bookcases in my room. A few of the other moms choked back giggles as Stephani hopped up. Clutching the baby, she raced out the door, past the angel-man named Jake—as in Jake Etsam, bassist of Jackaroo, the world's most famous band—toward the bathrooms at the end of the long hall.

"Guess that's a wrap for the day," Helena said, gathering up Ilona in her arms. The fifteen-month-old grunted, her eyes slamming shut. "You wore this one out, Ryn. Thanks for a great class of singing and songwriting," she said. The frown she threw over her shoulder at Jake did not register in the man's demeanor.

"Bye-bye!" Lionel shrieked. His mother, Kim, winced and smiled, her expression somewhere between apologetic and kill-me-now. "Transitions," she said.

"You're right, Lion-man. We didn't sing our goodbye song. You want a shaky egg to jam with?"

Lionel barreled through two other kids, sending them flying

as he dug into the egg basket, his mother chastising him and apologizing to the other moms at the same time.

Yeah, Jake Etsam, angel-man and rock god. This is *my* music scene. Deal with it.

I strummed out the chord and Lionel bounced, his diaper-clad tush mere inches from the carpet as he got busy to his favorite song. Ilona popped her head up and threw herself from her mother's arms to get in on the shaky-egg action. Samuel and Petey stopped crying as I started singing, each clapping and matching my pitch as we worked through each of their names to say goodbye.

"And hug your mommy tight. Bye-bye till next week," I said. I set my guitar in the middle of the floor, wincing a little as the remaining toddlers swarmed toward the polished wood, attacking the strings with their tiny fingers. This was their favorite part of the class and an easy way for the moms to pry the other chunky, plastic musical instruments from the kids' small hands.

"That's a custom-made Taylor," Jake choked. He'd moved behind me as we sang the final song. Well, the kids and I sang. The rest of the women eyed Jake's progress as he tiptoed around the edge of the classroom.

"I'd heard your brother was spending time in Seattle while his girlfriend recovered," Joan said. She was the oldest of our group—little Carina had been a surprise for Joan, her husband, and her high-school-aged daughter. She tucked her thick salt-and-pepper hair behind her ears as she set Carina down next to my guitar. The toddler cooed and slammed her palm against the strings.

"Fiancée," Jake replied, eyes still on the four toddlers climbing onto my guitar. "You're not worried about them breaking it?"

"Not really, no. They just want to look inside to see where the sound comes from."

"My daughter's a big fan of yours," Joan continued.

Jake raised startled eyes. Joan shook her head on a laugh. "Not this little cutie. My older daughter. She's a junior in high school."

"Oh, right-o. Want me to sign something for her?"

"Would you?" Joan asked, her smile blooming larger than I'd ever seen it. "That would just make Nicole's year."

"Course." Jake snagged a pen from the shelf behind me before grabbing an early-childhood music pamphlet and scrawling his name across the front. "Cheers." He handed the brochure to Joan, who clutched it to her chest. No way she was giving that to her daughter.

The other moms asked for his autograph, too. After another fifteen minutes, the toddlers had all lost interest in my guitar and two of them were bawling in earnest while Ilona and Petey rubbed their eyes and yawned.

"Nap time," Helena said. "Nice to meet you, Jake. Maybe if you stop by again, you can sing with Ryn. She has an amazing voice." Even I heard the reprimand in her words.

Jake dipped his head. "I know. Pulled me in with the first note."

My gaze darted back to his, and when our eyes locked, sincerity burned from the depths of his hazel eyes.

Lionel hugged my leg, breaking my intense contact with Jake. I ruffled Lionel's hair, then I waved a last goodbye to the ladies and kids. As they gathered their diaper bags and coats, I busied myself with wiping the toddler spittle from my guitar and setting it into its case.

"Er, I need to apologize."

My gaze darted back to Jake's. His cheeks and even his neck burned bright red but he kept his eyes firmly on mine. The intensity of his look slid over my body, making my skin warm and soften.

"I'm sorry if I offended you. I didn't mean…I just wasn't expecting…you know."

He stuttered through the apology. I shoved my hands into the back pockets of my jeans. *Of course* I knew who Jake Etsam was. *Of course* I was thrilled he'd sought me out. But that didn't mean I was going to let him trample over my work.

"No, I really don't," I said, shrugging. I snapped the last clasp of my guitar case closed and stood.

Jake ran his hand through his long brown waves. "I'm a wanker," he said, his voice a little lost. "I'm so sorry. Really. I should have thought before I…"

Stephani barreled back into the room, eyes wide. "I'm so glad you're still here!" Her eyes never left Jake's face even as she lowered Kendall to her feet. The nine-month-old's lip quivered but Stephani ignored her, racing to Jake's side and grabbing his arm. "I'm your biggest fan. Omigod! I can't believe I'm, like, touching you."

Jake inclined his head toward the now-sobbing Kendall. "What about your little girl?"

"She's not mine," Stephani said, frowning. "I just watch her. I'm totally single. Will you sign something for me? Want to grab some lunch? A drink? Go to the skating rink over at Westlake Center?"

I leaned my guitar against the wall and bent to pick up Kendall, whose whimpers ratcheted up to full-on wails. I cradled her in my arms and pressed my lips to her ear, singing a lullaby

I'd written last year as part of my healing process.

Kendall quieted enough for me to hear Stephani proposition Jake again. Yeah, Steph wasn't ever going to be on my faves list.

I patted Kendall's back and continued to croon, warmth building in my chest as the baby's pretty pink lips parted into a yawn. She looked up at me with her huge brown eyes. She reminded me of an owlet. She blinked, pressing her cheek into my chest.

"Oh, I'm sure Ryn won't mind keeping an eye on Kendall for a while. She loves kids." Stephani dismissed me without a second thought.

I did like Kendall quite a bit. But I wasn't going to change my afternoon plans so that Stephani could bag the sexy Aussie rocker.

Before I could tell her so, Jake smiled—well, it was more of a pained grimace—and sent me a pleading look.

"I'm on Ryn's calendar this arvo. And then I'm off to a meeting. Another time, perhaps."

"Oh. Well. Sure." Stephani's disappointment was palpable. Her eyes lit up. "Want me to show you all the cool places to party tonight? I'm dropping Kendall off at her mom's office around four."

I rolled my eyes but didn't stop singing. Kendall heaved a sigh and closed her eyes.

"Can't. I'm off to dinner at my brother's place. Private. Just family. Mila's still healing."

I chuckled into Kendall's hair. *Way to lay it on thick, angel-man.*

"Here you go, Steph. She's down for the count. Have a fun afternoon." I couldn't resist pressing a kiss to Kendall's soft, pink cheek. If it was anyone else, I would have gladly snuggled the baby for as long as I could. A pang bit through my chest as I swiped my thumb across Kendall's forehead, struggling with the longing I'd felt every time I looked at someone else's child.

This is what I lost when Desden didn't come home from his last tour in Iraq. We'd planned to start a family after I finished my master's degree. Instead, one night two years ago, three Army officers, in full dress attire, knocked on my apartment door to hand me Dez's medal of valor. He died in that war and I've been alone since.

I huffed out a breath and stepped back.

"You 'right?" Jake's voice softened as he stepped closer. Since his initial outburst, Jake had been considerate—not just of my feelings but of those of the ladies in my class.

"Yeah." I hoped. I'd learned grief hit like this—a sudden sucker punch to the chest. But I'd also learned to breathe through the intensity because I'd already come out the other side. Maybe scarred, but living my life nonetheless.

Such as it was. So different from what I'd hoped.

"Mila looks like that when she sees a baby. My brother's fiancée."I met Jake's concerned, intense hazel eyes. His hair tumbled into messy waves. Like he'd let it air dry after a morning surf. Or rolled out of a lover's bed.

Whoa. Where had that thought come from?

"I never lost a child, like Mila, if that's what you're getting at."

"Figured you knew who I am, read all the news about my family like the rest of the world," he said, his dimples flashing. They were deep wells bracketing his mouth like extra commas. Dez's dimples were smaller, just hints at humor. But, Jake, I'd bet, lived larger than my deceased war-hero husband ever had.

The pain settled low in my stomach, same as it did every time I heard of another's pregnancy. I'd begged Dez to try for our own child in the short months between his deployments. Often. He'd said he'd talk about baby matters when he returned from his next tour.

"Congratulations to your brother and his fiancée," I muttered.

He eyed me, aware of my less-than-enthusiastic response. "So that's why I'm here. Partly anyway. I heard your lullaby. It's gorgeous."

I'd had a fantasy of Dez's dark head singing to my growing bump. Well, except for the fact Dez barely held a tune, and he'd never been interested in music, preferring to kayak or rock climb—some physical outdoorsy activity that ate up his energy.

"Thanks."

Jake fidgeted, flustered by my lack of enthusiasm. "So, I thought, well, maybe you and I could sing it. I wanted to give it to Mila and Murphy as a wedding gift. They're getting married in February, weekend after Valentine's Day. Probably so Murphy doesn't fuck up and forget both."

I smiled, surprised by how touched I was by the thoughtfulness of the gesture. Jake Etsam might be a rock star, but he loved his family. I bet he'd make a great dad.

Flipping hyenas. I forced my eyes away from the all the gorgeous hotness standing in front of me. And that accent—swoon worthy—no wonder my ovaries had replaced my brain.

"That's sweet. So, you want to record the lullaby."

He fidgeted again. "I'd really like to sing with you. As a duet." His eyes darted around the room, his cheeks turning a ruddier hue. "But I don't sing, normally."

"You did back up on 'She's So Bad.'"

He smiled, probably thrilled I knew that. I almost rolled my eyes. Everyone knew Jackaroo. They were the band of the year—maybe the decade.

"Right-o. Also for 'Between Breaths.' But that's because both of those were on-the-fly, last-minute additions to the set list."

"You're kidding?" I gaped. I couldn't help it. "Those—both of those—are multiplatinum recordings!"

Jake shrugged, shoving his hands in his pockets. "Only bigger hit was 'Hold You Close,' which Murph insisted on singing solo. Those tunes are full of real emotion. That's what the fans respond to."

"On the fly?" I gasped, unable to comprehend his words afterward. But if Jake connected with my lullaby, then he'd felt the pent-up yearning in my song for the child I'd yet to meet.

"That may be overstating it. But point is, I'm not a singer, though I can carry a tune well enough. You are a singer. And I'd like to do an entire album for Mila. I think she'll like this as a gift, especially after everything she's been through in the past couple of years."

A sensitive, caring man. They weren't as rare as unicorns, but as much as I'd loved Dez, I had to admit he hadn't been the sensitive type. Unless…"Are you in love with her?" The question was sharp and inappropriate. Still, I wasn't helping a man steal his brother's pregnant lover.

"With Mila?" His eyes widened, turning greener than gold. I braced myself for him to say something scathing then turn and walk out. I rocked back on my heels, surprised when he shook his head, chuckling. "No. She's always been like my big sister. It's

133

just…Valentine's Day is her favorite holiday, and I want her to be, you know, happy. Because Murph is, and believe me, Murphy happy is a big deal. Fair dinkum."

Not quite sure about all that, but he seemed genuine. "Oh. Okay."

Those dimples popped back out. "Odd way to ask if I'm single."

"I wasn't." My cheeks flamed. "I just didn't want to help you romance away your brother's fiancée."

"With lullabies for my brother's bub?" He eyed me, a small smirk lingering at the corner of his mouth. "That'd be a new one."

"You're laughing at me," I huffed. His eyes crinkled at the corners. My chest burned, and I exhaled before I became too lightheaded. Dez was a handsome man, but Jake had looks and… presence. That's what made him so good of a performer. That I-don't-care-what-you-think vibe and sexy-as-sin smile.

"Because you're funny."

I picked up my guitar case and started toward the door, face flaming with embarrassment and inexplicable tears welling in my eyes.

"Wait." His voice filled with panic. "D-don't go," he stuttered.

I blinked back the tears—good at it after so much practice. "I'm not sure we have anything further to discuss."

"The song…maybe an album."

"I don't do vanity projects. I'm happy working with the early-childhood music program."

"This wouldn't be for vanity," he said with a gentle touch to my arm to turn me back toward him. "And I'm sure you're quite successful with your program. I've heard you sing." He smiled, those dimples flashing again, but his eyes remained uncertain.

I must stop melting each time he smiled. Who knew I had such a soft spot for *cheeks*?

"Thanks for popping in, Jake. Good luck with the project. I'll sign for the use of 'A Moonlit Serenade.'"

He grabbed the guitar case's handle, his warm hand sliding over mine. I jolted, letting go. My hand still tingled, the warmth drifting up my arm, into my chest, pooling low in my groin.

Fantastic. The first man I'd been attracted to *in years*, and he had to be a celebrity. One who managed to make me feel small and insignificant.

There was no way meeting Jake Etsam could end in anything other than embarrassment or heartache.